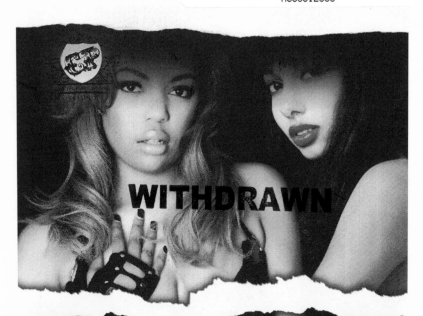

WITHDRAWN

YOUNG AND
DUMB
THE COMPLETE SERIES
DUCK SANCHEZ

Library of Congress Control Number: 2013939007
ISBN 10: 0984993096

ISBN 13: 9780984993093

Cover Design: Davida Baldwin www.oddballdsgn.com
Editor: Advanced Editorial Services
Graphics: Davida Baldwin
www.thecartelpublications.com
First Edition

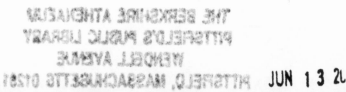

CHECK OUT OTHER TITLES BY THE CARTEL PUBLICATIONS

SHYT LIST 1: BE CAREFUL WHO YOU CROSS
SHYT LIST 2: LOOSE CANNON
SHYT LIST 3: AND A CHILD SHALL LEAVE THEM
SHYT LIST 4: CHILDREN OF THE WRONGED
SHYT LIST 5: SMOKIN' CRAZIES THE FINALE'
PITBULLS IN A SKIRT 1
PITBULLS IN A SKIRT 2
PITBULLS IN A SKIRT 3: THE RISE OF LIL C
PITBULLS IN A SKIRT 4: KILLER KLAN
POISON 1
POISON 2
VICTORIA'S SECRET
HELL RAZOR HONEYS 1
HELL RAZOR HONEYS 2
BLACK AND UGLY AS EVER
A HUSTLER'S SON 2
THE FACE THAT LAUNCHED A THOUSAND BULLETS
YEAR OF THE CRACKMOM
THE UNUSUAL SUSPECTS
MISS WAYNE AND THE QUEENS OF DC
LA FAMILIA DIVIDED
RAUNCHY
RAUNCHY 2: MAD'S LOVE
RAUNCHY 3: JAYDEN'S PASSION
REVERSED
QUITA'S DAYSCARE CENTER
QUITA'S DAYSCARE CENTER 2
DEAD HEADS
DRUNK & HOT GIRLS
PRETTY KINGS
HERSBAND MATERIAL
UPSCALE KITTENS
WAKE & BAKE BOYS
YOUNG & DUMB
THE END. HOW TO WRITE A BESTSELLING NOVEL IN 30 DAYS

What's Poppin' Fam,

This year has rolled by so fast, and we are already in May. Before you know it, 2013 will be gone and we will be on to a new year. But before I get ahead of myself, I'ma pause and be grateful for right now.

So far this year we have dropped seven novels. Seven books in five months is a good look, and that's only the beginning. So make sure you continue to hold us down, as we do this all for you.

Keeping in line with tradition, we want to send a special shout out to our friend and true boss:

Dr. LaTonja Martin

LaTonja Martin has her PhD in Mental Health and is currently the owner of Peaceful Haven Inc., a non-profit organization that services the community in the DMV (DC, Maryland and Virginia) area. With six homes in her organization, she cares for many people, including veterans who have fought for our country, but may need a little assistance. Not only is she giving back to the community, but she is a beautiful person and the Cartel Publications loves her to pieces.

Aight, get to it! I'll see you in the next novel. ;)

Be Easy!
Charisse "C. Wash" Washington
Vice President
The Cartel Publications
www.thecartelpublications.com
www.twitter.com/cartelbooks
www.facebook.com/cartelpublications

CHAPTER 1

BOBBI

Once Upon A Time In Washington DC, lived a nasty mouthed young woman...

The sun produced a heat so strong during the morning that Bobbi nearly lost her mind. "Fuck you, you dirty dick, stank breath, no job having bastard," seventeen year old Bobbi Gannon yelled, as she stood butt naked in front of her boyfriend Red's apartment building.

Her meaty butt cheeks jiggled, and the nipples of her small breasts rose to attention. By all accounts she looked a hot mess, but you couldn't tell her that.

Although she was angry, the reason she was set out like yesterday's trash was all her fault. Bobbi made the mistake of going through Red's iPhone when he was in the shower, to see whom he was cheating with on the side. She got exactly what she was looking for, her feelings hurt. Sure enough it was his ex-girlfriend Nia from up the block, who he swore he wasn't feeling anymore. But had she took the time to put her clothes on before moving on the sneak tip, she wouldn't be in front of his ground floor apartment playing herself

6

royally. Instead she was giving everybody in Southeast DC, a free peep show.

At least one thing good could be said about Bobbi, if anything at all, her body was on point. Her caramel complexion sparkled under the yellow sun, and she was sweating so hard it looked like she'd just stepped out of a pool.

"I hate you so much," she continued to scream.

"I love you too, Bobbi," Red joked, tossing her blue jeans and pink shirt to her feet from his window. "Now get the fuck from 'round my spot, before I tell you how I really feel." He threw her purse in her face and her phone fell out and toppled to the ground. "You got my neighbors out here in my business and shit." He looked around at the audience she collected with her little performance.

"Nigga, I'm dead serious"— she eased into her jeans—"if you don't let me back into the house I'm not fucking with you no more. It's over for real! No pussy, no calling me, no dick sucking, no nothing." She ran her fingers through her short curly auburn hair, thinking it was all out of place. "Now open the door before I go off."

"Bobbi, you not paying attention, your pussy is done over here! I been looking for a reason to stop fucking with your young, dumb ass. Leave it to you to give me a reason by going through my shit. That's why you out there, and I'm in the cool air-conditioning about to crack open a cold beer. Now kick rocks, bitch!" He slammed the window closed.

"I fucking hate you!" She pulled her shirt angrily over her head, forcing her neck to the side. "You hear me, I fucking hate you!" She snatched her purse up off the ground and stuck her tongue out at everybody who was looking at her with disapproving eyes.

"Congratulations because you really playing yourself out here today," somebody said behind her. "But that's what you get when you fuck somebody on the first date."

Although Bobbi knew the person was right, and that she had no intentions on giving up the goodies so early in the future, she would never let her know.

When she saw Red's ex-girlfriend staring at her she rolled her eyes. "Don't look at me, monkey." She brushed the grass off of her cell phone. "Don't even act like he didn't do the same shit to you too, when he chose me. Remember? You were banging on the door, begging him to take you back and everything." She slid her feet into her black flip-flops.

"The only thing is he opened the door back for me to let me put my clothes on. You been out here for"— she looked at her watch— "5 minutes and counting. Damn, Bobbi, I guess you should've married that nigga that proposed to you six months ago, at least he wanted something to do with your funky ass."

"And you should've let Lin Lee shave more corn off of that waxy toe you, bum bitch!"

After reading the chick her rights, Bobbi stormed down the street just as angry as she wanted to be. She wasn't with Red long, but he was the only man who let her stay in his apartment when he wasn't home and she fucked that up. He was the one who brought her McDonald's to her high school when she got the munchies. He was the one who bought her, her first designer handbag, which made everybody in her school jealous, until word got out that it was fake and she got it from New York. Had she just respected the relationship, and left well enough alone, she may have lasted until the summer. But Bobbi was a confused girl who wanted everything without giving an honest effort.

She wanted someone to take care of her, even though she didn't respect those who loved her. She wanted money, even though she didn't bother to get a job. She wanted someone she could believe in even though she was untrustworthy, and often dishonest. She went about life feeling she deserved the best, although she gave nothing in return.

"Pookie, please tell me why Reds just threw me out of his apartment," Bobbi said walking down the street, as she spoke to her cousin on the cell phone. "Bitch, I felt like punching that nigga in the face but I couldn't get to him. 'Cause he was hiding behind the window. I should throw a rock in that bitch right now!"

"Let me guess, you went through his phone and found out he was fucking with Nia again?"

"Girl, how did you know?" she stopped walking.

"Because when you told me you were going through his shit, I told you not to get caught." She laughed. "You know he leaves the shower on even when he's done just to run out of the bathroom and catch you in the act. Remember, that's how you got caught going through his wallet too."

"Fuck all that"— she started walking again— "can you come get me? I don't have no money on me and I need a ride."

"A ride where? Your mother is done with you."

"I guess to your house." She shrugged.

Pookie sighed. "Yes, girl, where are you now?"

Bobbi looked at the street signs. "Naylor and Good Hope Road. In front of the Kentucky Fried Chicken."

"Well go inside and get something to eat. I know you hungry. I'll be there when I can."

"Didn't you hear me say I don't have no money. I need you to hurry up and scoop me, Pookie, for real. My head hurt."

"Bitch, don't rush me. You the one out Southeast acting all dumb and shit. Like I said, I'll be there in five minutes."

Bobbi pulled the door open to the restaurant, and slammed her ass into a red plastic seat. She waited five minutes, and then fifteen minutes, but still Pookie hadn't showed up in her old white Tahoe. Since her lips felt dry, she over applied her clear lip-gloss to make her mouth sparkle.

After thirty more minutes, and constant trips to the door to see if her cousin had come, she called Pookie back but she didn't answer the phone. An hour later she was fuming mad. *I knew that bitch was going to set me up out here!*

With nothing better to do, she grabbed a pile of straws and started pulling them out of the paper wrappings and throwing them on the table in front of her. With no money in her pocket, she had no idea what she was going to do. Not only that, her mother told her since she kept fucking with Reds, even though she asked her not to, she was not welcome into her home. She promised her that one day she was going to meet the wrong person, and when she did, she would be changed forever. The only problem was, Bobbi never listened and as a result she was essentially homeless.

"You must be bored," somebody said standing over top of her. "Come with me and I'll give you something to do."

When she looked up, she saw the sexiest nigga she had ever seen. He was 6'2, with real neat long cornrows running down his back. His thick eyebrows showcased his dark brown eyes, and she could tell by the black Jordan throwback sweat suit and gold chain hanging around his neck that he had money.

Grinning like a dog getting its belly rubbed Bobbi said, "You don't even know me. How you know I'm bored?"

"Because anybody taking straws out of wrappers and throwing them on the table must not have enough to do with her time." He put his hand out. "You coming with me or what?"

Bobbi eventually got a hold of Pookie on the phone, and she let her know how she felt for leaving her up KFC. After enduring ten minutes of verbal abuse from her, Pookie said she was sorry but that she couldn't pick her up, because her son's father took her car and crashed it into a mailbox while drunk. He got arrested, and she had to catch a cab home. She said she could come over her house if she could get a ride, and Vyce promised to drop her off, but first he had to go to the hotel and freshen up.

He was in the shower washing up, and Bobbi was sitting on the bed looking around the room. There was something about men's clothing that made her smile. She couldn't stop looking at his Jordan's and how neat and clean they were. She loved men who knew how to dress and Vyce Anderson certainly fit the picture. She just turned the TV on when Vyce called her name.

"Bobbi, can you come in here for a minute, I need the soap. I could get it myself but I don't want to slip on the floor."

She slowly strolled toward the bathroom and opened the door. The soap was sitting on the sink, and from where she stood it looked like it was wet. Like he just used it, and put it back but she couldn't be sure.

"Here you go," she reached into the shower curtain with the soap bar, but turned her head to prevent seeing him naked. "I'll see you when you come out." She moved for the door.

"Ouch," Vyce yelled. "Damn, it! I can't see!"

"What's wrong?" she turned back toward the shower curtain, but didn't walk close.

"I got soap in my eyes, and can't see my joint. I hate when this shit happens. I might need your help."

"You okay?" she inched just a little closer.

"Yeah, but I know this sounds weird, and I'm not trying to come at you wrong, because I really like you. But I need you to wash my joint for me because the soap in my eyes burns. So I can't clean myself right. Can you help me?"

Awkward silence filled the bathroom.

Something in her gut said that he was trying to play her, but what if he wasn't? Then she wouldn't be able to get a ride home or make a new friend.

"What exactly do you want me to wash, Vyce?" she was chagrined.

"Come on, Bobbi, you not going to make me say it are you? I'm embarrassed enough already that I gotta even come at you like this. Don't make me feel worse by going all the way."

She knew exactly what he wanted...his dick cleaned. "But...I don't understand why you can't do it yourself?"

He sighed. "You know what, I really liked you, but since you gonna act like a kid, and don't even want to help a nigga out, you can just leave my hotel room. That's why I don't deal with young bitches. They too insecure and not mature enough."

"But I don't have no way to get home!" she stomped.

"Call your people if you want, that's on you. But I want you out of my room right now. Bounce!"

Bobbi was in a serious bind now. If she left the hotel room, she would have to call a million people to take her to her cousin's. She burned so many bridges that she couldn't think of one soul, outside of her cousin, who was in her corner. And the worst part was that she really liked Vyce. If she left like this, he may never want to see her again.

"Okay, I'll do it," she sighed.

She walked up to the shower curtain and pulled it back, revealing his sexy body. Vyce worshiped the gym and it showed. His abs were chiseled and muscles were pronounced everywhere you could see. He was by all accounts perfect.

"That's, my sweet baby." He handed her the soap. "Go ahead, I don't bite."

Bobbi held the soap in one hand and his dick in the other. Rubbing the soap along the length of his dick, she watched as white suds cover his stiffening brown stick. When Vyce started moaning she could feel herself creaming her pants. Although his eyes were suddenly open, and it was clear that he could do it himself, she decided to go with the show. Besides, she was suddenly horny and wanted him inside of her anyway.

"Hey, Bobbi, kiss it for me with them pretty lips." He ran this thumb over her bottom lip and stuck it into her mouth. It rested on her wet tongue. Instinctively she suckled it like a nipple.

"Ughh, Vyce, I can't do that." She continued with his thumb in her mouth. "I don't even know you like that yet."

"Bobbi, I'm gonna be real with you," he said while she still held onto his dick like a hand. "I think you the kind of bitch I want to be serious about. But if you gonna fake on me, and not step up to be the kind of woman I need, I'm gonna start thinking you not the one. I mean, don't you like me as much as I like you?"

"Yes!"

"Don't you want to push my Benz, while I sit in the passenger seat? Or use my ride whenever you need it?"

"For real," she asked. "You'll let me drive your car?"

"For real. But we can't have that type of relationship if you not one hundred with me. So how about you kiss it for me, and then get in here to take a shower with me."

With the future etched out in her mind, Bobbi's knees slammed against the porcelain floor, so quickly they almost fractured. Vyce used a few halfhearted words and it worked. Her mother always said she was young and dumb, but Bobbi felt she didn't understand her properly. Her mother was old, in her thirties, and not smart like she was. Bobbi couldn't even count the number of times men would be in and out of her mother's life, leaving her with a broken heart, and soggy pussy. In her opinion her mother knew nothing, and she didn't care what she thought and as a result their relationship was strained.

"Yeah, just like that, Bobbi," he moaned as he fucked her face. "Yeah, that's, my sweet baby. Lick it, lick it just like that." He looked down at her. He was an awesome coach. "Open that mouth, Bobbi. Open it real wide."

He liked her instantly, because she did everything he asked, despite not being able to breathe as he forced his stiffness down her throat. When he felt he was about to nut he stopped her. He was greedy and he wanted some of that pussy too. "Bobbi, take your jeans off, I want to fuck you from the back."

She yanked off her clothes and slid out of her wet panties so quickly even if he wanted to change his mind he couldn't. She stepped into the tub, and placed her hands on the wall like she was under arrest. Before she knew it he filled her up with 9 inches of raw dick. Vyce was relentless as he pounded the young girl's loins and she took every bit of it too. The entire time she was thinking, *this is my man, and I'm his bitch*.

Before Bobbi realized it, she had a pussy full of nut.

When he was done he said, "I fucking love you, girl. Do you hear me, you got my heart now." He kissed her lips and she grinned. "See that's why I like young girls, your pussy stay tight and fresh. Them old bitches can't fuck like ya'll can. Man, I swear you gonna make me cut everybody off just to be with you." He hopped out of the shower and wrapped a towel around his waist. "You stay in here and keep that thing wet for me. I'm gonna grab us a couple of wine coolers and come finish you off. You with that, my sweet baby?"

"I'll be waiting!"

Realizing she caught a keeper, Bobbi began spinning around in the tub and singing her heart out. But after fifteen minutes, the water ran cold and he hadn't returned. She wondered where he went.

She turned the water off and yelled, "Vyce!" He didn't answer. "Vyce, where you at?"

When he didn't respond she walked out of the bathroom naked, only to find those Jordan's she thought were so sexy gone.

CHAPTER 2

CLAIRE

Later on in a kitchen within the suburbs of Mary-land, a young woman took verbal abuse from her mother…

"I know you think I'm being hard on you, Claire, but it's only because I love you," Ricky Dixon said to her only child, "and if you don't hear this from me, who else you gonna hear it from?"

Ricky was putting long black box braids into her friend Nixon's hair. Although she owned four braiding salons in and around the DMV (DC, Maryland and Virginia) area she invited her best friends over to her home to be serviced.

"If you love me so much, how come it don't feel like it sometimes?" Seventeen-year-old Claire Dixon asked, her natural curly shoulder length hair, snatched back into a ponytail. "You always saying I can't do this, and I can't do that. Like you don't believe in me or something. The teacher at my school said I can be anything I want to in life."

"Excuse me, Ricky, but I gotta talk to your daughter for a second." Nixon interjected. "Claire, you and I both know you are immature. Now I know you don't mean to be, but that's what it is."

Claire hated Nixon the most out of her mother's friends. She always felt comfortable butting in her business, and her mother never stopped her. In Claire's opinion she didn't know enough about her life to tell her what to do with it. Besides, she also gave bad advice.

Like the time she told her to go to her school and tell her only friend that she thought she was jealous of her, because she kept embarrassing her in front of other people in the cafeteria. This did nothing but make Fish angry, and stop talking to her permanently. So Claire didn't believe anything Nixon said, and she hated the tone of her voice.

"You don't even know me like that." Claire sat on the barstool. "You only know what my mama tell you." She grabbed her cell phone off the counter, and scrolled through her Flickgram page.

"I don't have to know you like that, young lady, and you need to mind your tongue when you're talking to grown folks. That's part two of your problem."

"She's right, Claire, don't get sassy," Ricky added.

Claire rolled her eyes.

"Now I might not live here, but I was here when you let your so called friends come over, and they ended up stealing over ten thousand dollars of your mother's jewelry." She shook her finger at Claire, and she wanted to break it. "Or what about the time you lost your key while your mother was on vacation, and had to call me off my good government job just to let you in?" she paused. "You need to get your life together and you need to do it now. You gonna end up meeting the wrong person."

"Claire, do you even know what you want out of life," Ricky asked. "Because as of now you seem confused. I know you experienced real heartache recently, but its time to move on."

Claire sighed. "I know what I want, mama, but you just gonna laugh if I tell you." She placed her phone on the counter. "So I'm not going to even say anything."

"What is it?"

"I want a baby, somebody I can take care of."

Ricky's eyes widened. "You can't be that stupid! You can't even take care of yourself! You are single handedly the most irresponsible person I know. How the fuck you gonna take care of a child?"

Claire pouted. "It's what I want, mama, you asked me remember?"

"You know what, I'm done talking to you at this point." She stopped braiding, grabbed her purse and handed Claire a fifty-dollar bill. "Go to the beauty supply store and get me a pack of 1B braiding hair. And hurry up back because I'm almost finished this side of her head and will be moving to the next."

Claire moved quickly out of the stool, trying to get far away from her mother anyway. "Okay, ma, but can I take your car?"

"Take your own car and hurry up back."

Claire trudged out of the door with her purse in hand. On the way to her car, she ran into Packs, her ex boyfriend, who lived in the neighborhood. She saw his light skin and coal black eyes approaching before he reached her. Although she told herself that she didn't love him anymore, it didn't stop her from still caring about him. Packs was her first love, but he made a mistake of breaking her heart on a day she could never forget, although she often tried.

"How are things going, Claire?" he stepped to her car. "You still mad at me? I mean, can you ever forgive me?"

Claire opened the door to her gold Jeep without responding.

"The least you can do is say hello," he said. "Don't we mean anything to each other anymore? Don't you want to come back to me? And be with me forever, like we talked about?"

She slid in her seat, slammed the car door and pulled off. She went down the road some ways, and when she looked in her rearview mirror he was gone. When she felt herself crying uncontrollably, she turned the radio on as loud as possible. She was trying to drown out the sound of her own sobs but it wasn't working.

All her life she was emotional, and felt she took things way too seriously. But how could she change? When Packs was in her corner, she was happy because his neediness made her feel loved, and time flew by when they were together. Now things had changed and she was frustrated and lonely.

When her truck stuttered, and stopped her eyes spread. She looked at the console and noticed the yellow gas tank signal was flashing brightly. It had been on before she entered the car, but she felt she could make the next two lights to the station up the road like she'd always done. But once again she thought wrong.

She went for her phone until she realized she left it at home on the kitchen counter. This was exactly the type of thing her mother was talking about that she wasn't trying to hear. She was irresponsible to the fifth degree, and this was proof positive. Even if she could call her mother to tell her she ran out of gas, she wouldn't because she didn't feel like hearing her mouth.

Not knowing what else to do, she got out, popped the hood of the car and looked at the engine. Everything looked like it was written in French and she had no idea what she was doing. Figuring she could make it up the street to the gas station, if the engine cooled down, she blew small cold puffs from her mouth, and over it. The entire thing from a far looked foolish.

She was almost out of breath until someone said, "What you doing, ma?"

When she turned her head, she saw a man with long corn rolls down his back, wearing a black Jordan sweat suit. He was sitting behind the driver's seat of his car. He was the sexiest man she'd ever seen in her life, and she wanted him for herself immediately. When her eyes rolled over the silver Mercedes E-Class Benz, she almost pooped her pants but she tried to hold it together. He was rich, she could tell it!

"I ran out of gas"— she looked at his lips— "so I was trying to—"

"Blow kisses at it?" he chuckled.

She giggled and then shrugged. "I guess that's what it looked like right?"

"Look, how about you ride with me right quick to make a stop, and I'll take you to get a can and some gas. Will that be cool?" he looked at his watch. "I mean I got some place to be, but I don't want to leave you out here by yourself, ma. I'd never be able to live with myself."

Claire was hesitant because she never dealt with somebody as obviously rich and as old as him before. Plus she didn't know if he was some sick crazed rapist. So she looked at him before answering. Since he hadn't bothered to get out of the car she observed his eyes and the thick eyebrows she loved on a man. She decided that he could possibly change her life, or at least give her some gas, and either would be appreciated at the moment.

"That'll be cool, if you don't mind," Claire said. "But I can't be out long, my mama is expecting some braiding hair for one of her clients. And the last thing I feel like is hearing her mouth."

"I got you, my sweet baby," he winked. He popped the locks to the car. "Get inside, where it's nice and cool."

Claire was slightly irritated and nervous. She knew her mother was cursing up a storm right now since she didn't come straight back with the hair like she was supposed too. Plus she didn't understand why she had to go to Vyce's hotel room, just so he could take her to get some gas later. And since she saw the word BITCH written on the mirror in pink lipstick when she first walked in, she figured another female had been there even though the bed was still made up. She wanted to ask him but he was so serious about taking a shower that she decided to wait.

She was sitting on the bed watching TV when Vyce yelled, "Claire, can you come here for a second?"

"For what?" she yelled back. *Set It Off* with Queen Latifah just came on, and she wanted to watch it, since she could never catch it from the beginning. "I'm watching TV!"

"I left the soap on the bathroom sink, you mind handing it to me?"

Claire looked at the bathroom door and frowned. "Uhhhh…you're in there by yourself, just walk out and get it, I won't see you."

"It'll help me out big time if you can bring it to me. It's just on the sink, and it ain't like I'll bite you or something."

"No," she said rolling her eyes. "I don't come into strange bathrooms and give men I don't know like that soap." She continued to focus on the TV. "Just get it yourself."

A few more minutes passed and he yelled, "Ouch!"

She leaped off of the bed and walked to the closed door. "Are you okay in there? Did you fall or something?"

"Can you come in here right quick, Claire? I got some soap in my eyes and this shit is burning like crazy."

"I'm not a doctor, Vyce. I mean you in the tub and all. Just splash some cool water in your face and get it out. You'll be fine."

"Help a nigga out, Claire. Please. Why you gotta be so cold?"

After waiting about a minute, she reluctantly opened the door and walked inside of the bathroom. Sure enough his freak nasty ass was inside the shower with the curtains wide open, and his face covered in white suds. *Wow, he really goes all out to fuck a girl doesn't he?* She thought.

"Can you wash, my joint, man I can't see it."

Claire looked at him and his dick like he was crazy. Although his body was like no other, he was playing himself and that turned her off. "Wait, are you asking me if I can wash your penis for you because you have soap in your eyes?"

"Yeah, you gonna help me or not?"

Claire laughed so hard; she fell on the slippery floor. Instead of giving attention to the pain that ran up her backbone, she was holding her gut. She felt he had the whackest game known to man, and she couldn't believe he tried it on her. There he was, a sudsy face, limp penis, mess.

"What the fuck is so funny?" he asked. He ran his face under the water and opened his eyes.

"It's a miracle," she yelled. "You can see."

"Man, fuck you. I really did have soap in my face you know. I don't gotta run no game on no bitch to fuck."

"Oh, my God, you can't be serious. Please tell me the girl who wrote that shit on the mirror, didn't fall for that weak game. Please tell me she had enough sense to know when somebody was playing her or not."

Embarrassed, he rinsed the suds off of his body while she continued to laugh at his expense. When he was done he turned the water off in an effort to get as far away from her as possible.

Claire didn't care that he was butt ass naked in the tub, this was the best laugh she had all day and she needed it.

"You can get up now," he said, feeling humiliated. He stepped out of the shower and placed one of the towels around his waist, like he had earlier that day when he was with Bobbi. Except this time his plan didn't work, and he didn't get any pussy. "It ain't even all that funny." He helped her off the floor and walked her out of the bathroom.

"Yes it is…oh my God!" she sat on the edge of the bed and examined how angry he looked as he put his clothes on. "You too fine to be doing all that dumb shit. If you wanna fuck a girl you should just ask her. But the soap in the eyes routine? Really? That was so lame!" when she saw his eyebrows drawn together in anger she settled down. "Why you mad?"

"Because you over there acting like a nigga over here opening up for Kevin Hart or something. You don't even know me like that."

"I'm sorry," she said wiping her tears. His anger was adorable. "Please, come sit down next to me." He continued to lace up his sneakers. "Vyce, please. Sit down for one second." He walked over to the bed, and slammed his ass down like a spoiled kid. "Can we start all over again? Without all of the stunts and shows?"

"How?" he asked looking into her pretty face.

"Like this"— she extended her hand— "Hi, my name is Claire, and your name is?"

"Vyce." He shook her hand.

"Vyce, it's a pleasure to meet you."

He smiled for the first time since he saw her giggling. "It's a pleasure to meet you too, ma." He shook his head. "Look, all that shit just now got me hungry, want to get something to eat?"

"Yes."

"What you like?"

"My favorite is Chinese Food." She smiled.

He ordered out and they spent the next two hours talking and drinking cheap wine in the room. He asked her about what she wanted out of life, and she didn't bother to tell him she wanted a child. Because she knew enough to know men steered clear away from females like that. When Claire was buzzing, and her eyes lowered, he decided to go at her again.

"Look, I really like you." He rubbed her curly ponytail backwards. "You're the first female who ever put me in my place. And I'm gonna say something else to you, because I want to always be honest with you. I ran that game on at least fifteen bitches, and every one but you failed." That part was true. "That tells me something about you. You're a grade 'A' type of female and I need somebody like you in my life. Somebody to keep me grounded."

"Stop playing, Vyce," she said, although she hoped what he was saying was authentic. There was something about his eyes that told her he was being honest now.

"I'm serious, mami. I'm feeling you big time. Do you realize I had something to do today, but I dropped all of that, just to hang out with you? Even though you made me mad at first." He playfully jabbed her jaw.

"So now what?" she asked, hoping he'd jump out there and ask her to be his girl, like Packs did on their first date.

"I don't know," he shrugged. "But let's start with a kiss."

He released her long curly hair from the ponytail holder. Then he pulled her chin softly toward him, and planted a kiss on the corner of her mouth. Then he did the other corner before pressing against her soft lips. Within the hour she was naked, and he was inside of her body...*raw*. To hear Claire tell it, it was the best sexual experience of her life, and one she would always remember.

She went to sleep in his arms and woke up hugging a pillow as the sunshine peeked in the window.

But just like he did Bobbi, he left her alone.

CHAPTER 3

VYCE

(TWO MONTHS LATER)

On the deck of a million dollar home...

"So you know my first baby's mom is beefing with me again right?" Whiz asked Vyce, as they sat in the back of his home in Virginia, on the deck. The sun was bright and a perfect breeze blew everywhere.

"What she do this time?"

"She thinks I should give her more money than I already do." He shook his head. "Vyce, this bitch gets two thousand dollars for my youngest daughter, and an extra five hundred just so she can stay off of my back."

"And extra five hundred? What's wrong with you, man?" Vyce leaned in. "You fucking up the game for everybody with that move. You're supposed to pay what the law says, not a penny more." He stabbed his finger on the table.

Whiz was Vyce's best friend. Although he was white he preferred black women, believing there was something exotic about them. His piercing blue eyes, blond hair and inviting smile made him a favorite with the sisters. But just like black men, he proved to think with the head between his legs instead of the one on top. But if there was one thing that could be said about Whiz, it was that he took care of his children.

As his youngest daughter, seven-year-old Noodles wiggled in his lap, he picked her up and placed her down. "Baby, go over there to the pool with your sister. I'm talking to uncle Vyce now."

"She don't like me to play with her when she thinking," she whined. "She throws water in my face and makes my eyes burn."

Whiz focused on his thirteen year old daughter who was swimming without a care in the world, since her younger sister was out of her way. "Nooch, I'm sending Noodles back over there to get in the pool. So stop teasing her. I got company."

"Why she gotta come over here, daddy?" she yelled. "I'm chilling right now."

"Either do what I say or I'm taking your phone away! Which one you want?"

"Ughhh, I can't stand you," she yelled at her sister.

Having gotten her way, Noodles switched all the way over to her sister, with full intentions of getting on her nerves.

"Man, your daughters are beautiful," Vyce admitted. "That's one thing I know for sure. Black and white people sure do make some beautiful children together. Ya'll just don't be taking all the sisters."

"All the sisters?" he chuckled." As many white women that ya'll have stolen? If anything it's our turn, man."

"Yeah, whatever," Vyce responded, only half serious. "Ya'll been fucking our women since the slavery days!"

Whiz laughed. "Anyway, things would be sweet as far as my kids are concerned, if only I could get both of my daughter's mothers to act right." He shook his head. "I would've saved money had I let both of them stay in my house like they wanted."

Vyce almost choked after that comment. "What you talking about? Two black women live here? Together?"

"I'm serious, Diane and Erica wanted to stay here, man. They promised to get along and everything and had I let them, I would've saved about five thousand dollars a month. I can't buy shit now because if I do, I have to worry about them wanting half. I revisited the offer last month and they rescinded. Saying they good now. I guess it's because they fucking with new men."

"Man, they would've killed each other had that shit went down. I don't care what you say."

"Maybe," he shrugged, "but then I wouldn't have had to pay child support. It would've been a win-win situation for all of us." He picked up his beer and took a large sip. "Anyway, what's up with the real estate deal in Texas? You in or what? Because it would be a shame for you to let it go to waste. You gonna come out good in the end."

"I don't know, man. The whole idea of putting a million dollars on a property, under the pretenses of getting money in the future doesn't jive too well with me. I mean how do I know for sure this inside track you have is fool proof?"

"First of all you a drug dealer. And outside of the homes, and the mobile spots you got around DC, you not doing anything real with your money. A million dollars is nothing to you, and you and I both know it." He paused. "You might as well invest."

"Them little mobile spots you talking about earn me a five hundred thousand dollars in sales a year," Vyce told him.

"And I'm talking about making multi-millions. It ain't even a real investment for you. One million on this property will triple your money. They are turning that area into a stadium, man. And when they start to build it out, they'll have to come to you to buy the property you own. You write your own ticket."

"If this idea is so sweet, why aren't you getting involved?"

"Are you even listening to me? Because if either of my children's mothers find out I'm stepping into real estate, it will be like I never owned it to begin with. They'll take me for every cent I'm worth. The only thing they know is that I push prescription meds to a few college kids, and that's' all they need to know. I'll tell you, man, be glad you don't have no kids."

The moment he said that, Vyce's phone rang. The number was blocked so he frowned and said, "Who this?"

"It's me, Claire."

His eyes widened because he never gave her his contact information. "Hold up, how you get my cell number?"

"I guess you should be surprised, considering how you left the hotel room in a hurry and all, just after making love to me two months ago. All that stuff about caring about me was all bullshit. You good, Vyce, real good."

He grinned. "Whatever."

"Here's the thing, you good but I'm better. Because as you can see, I found you."

He cleared his throat. "Look, I'm sorry about the way I left, my peoples called and there was an emergency. I had to split. Remember I told you I had something to do when I first scooped you up, so I ended up having to take care of it in the morning."

"It's okay."

"So what's up, I know you didn't call me two months later just to tell me you still mad at me. " He had a few minutes to spare and wasn't doing anything so he decided chilling with her couldn't hurt much. Besides, she was great in bed. "You trying to hook up or something?"

"No."
"Then what you want?"
"To tell you that I'm pregnant."

CHAPTER 4

CLAIRE

Three hours later at a small diner in Washington DC...

Claire watched Vyce stab at his steak and eggs like he hadn't eaten a day in his life. She was a little jealous because although his appetite was intact, the meaty scent of the chicken in front of her did nothing but cause her stomach to churn. She had no idea that this pregnancy would be so rough, but she quickly learned.

"Vyce, can we finally talk," she asked softly. "We been here for thirty minutes and you haven't said anything to me yet."

He continued to poke at his food until every last morsel was down his throat and resting in the pit of his stomach. When he was done he wiped the corners of his mouth with a napkin, sucked his teeth and said, "It ain't mine."

Her eyes widened and she leaned in. "What you mean it ain't mine?"

"Just what I said, shawty," he threw the napkin on the table. "You gave up the pussy too easy for it to be mine. I can't believe you would even come at me like

36

this, considering how loose you was back in that hotel."

Claire's heart rocked in her chest and she was trying to steady her breathing. In all of her life she'd never been so humiliated. She didn't know what she expected him to say, but she hoped he'd at least admit to getting her pregnant. At the most, maybe with a little time, he would want to be a father.

Vyce proved to be the most interesting man she'd ever encountered. When he was having sex with her, and said he loved her in her ear, even though he just met her, she believed him. He was that good. It was the only reason she allowed him to nut inside of her body, as she whispered I love you back. Now she felt like such a fool. He was different. Different in his interaction with her, and she didn't understand why.

"Vyce, I'm sorry if I gave you the wrong impression about me"— she wiped the tears away from her eyes— "but I meant it when I said I love you, and I hoped you meant it when you said you loved me too. Or do you just run around DC telling girls you love them when you really don't?"

"I didn't say I love you," he lied.

"But you did." She placed her hand over her heart. "You told me when we were making love. Don't you remember? You told me how good I smelled and how tight my pussy was. Why you doing this to me, Vyce?"

He laughed. "Listen, all I know is this, that baby you carrying around ain't mine. Now if you want to be

37

up in here, fronting like it's mine then you wasting your fucking time."

"But you didn't use a condom!"

"I never use a condom." He laughed. "I like to feel the pussy when I'm inside. Them things don't do nothing but make my dick dry." He separated a stick of gum from a pack, took one out and stuffed the pack back inside his pocket. All without offering her one piece. "Look, you a cutie. You really are. And I can tell by how tight that pussy was that you wasn't fucking often. Now I'm not calling you a freak, or nothing but something is off here." He popped the piece of gum into his mouth. "There's no way in the world I could've gotten you pregnant that quick."

With a red face she asked, "But how do you know?"

"Because I had a CAT Scan on my head." He pointed at his braids. "And whenever men have CAT Scan's it makes them unable to have children. See what I'm saying?"

"I don't understand, Vyce? But...I haven't been with nobody else."

"See that's why I don't like dealing with young girls," he lied. "You throw the coochie around and then when you don't get your way, you try to press a baby on a nigga."

The truth was, Vyce preferred the young girls. Whenever he was around them he was able to tell them the most ridiculous of stories, and they'd believe him wholeheartedly. He told another girl about having a CAT Scan and she believed he was right. He was so good that to this day a boy child who looked like him was walking around the world, with no father figure in his life. He was king deadbeat.

"Now I'll give you some money to have an abortion, because I'm a good dude"— he reached into his pocket, grabbed his wallet and removed four hundred dollars— "you can take yourself to the clinic on Pennsylvania Avenue and have them get you together." He threw the money at her and it landed on the chicken on her plate. "But I can't do nothing else for you." He stood up. "You ready to go?"

"Have you ever been in love, Vyce? Because if you let me, I can love you."

He frowned. "I knew you were weird."

She gritted her teeth. "My mother wants me to ask, how successful is Vyce Communications? She said she read somewhere that the company is worth a half a million. Tell me, Vyce, is that true?" she looked up at him. "Me and my baby are going to need the financial support and it's good to know."

When he heard the name of his highly successful mobile phone company, he farted. "What...what you talking about?"

She looked around to see who was looking at them. Then she whispered and said, "Sit down, Vyce."

He did.

"When my mother learned that I was pregnant by you, needless to say she was angry. Now I don't know much about this CAT Scan stuff, and I'll ask my mother when I—"

"I'd appreciate if you don't tell your mother about me not being able to have children due to having a CAT Scan." He said with an attitude. "It's very private." Really he was embarrassed and knew an adult would rip his head off if they heard anything so ridiculous. "You owe me at least that much since you up and got yourself pregnant."

She didn't know why, but she agreed to keep his secret. "Okay, but we still have a problem. What are *we* going to do about *our* baby?"

He sighed. "I'm gonna be real with you, when you first called me I was happy."

"Why?" she smiled slightly.

"Because it bothered me that I left you the way I did, and I wanted a chance to make it right. But if we are going to get to know each other, you gonna have to get rid of that baby, Claire. I'm not ready for no kids. I'm only thirty years old. I'm still young."

"My mother—"

"That's what I'm talking about, this is between me and you. Your mother threatening me, by mentioning my companies makes me uncomfortable. Now if you don't want the possibility of getting to know me better, tell me now, and I'll leave you to it."

"I do, so much, Vyce," she said with hopeful eyes.

40

"Then prove it to me, Claire. Get an abortion." He stood up again and reached his hand out. "Let's go get a hotel, and spend some time with each other. Just me and you. I promise not to leave you this time. I just want to hold you in my arms."

"For real?" she accepted his hand and stood up.

"Yeah, and since you didn't eat your food, probably because you have a sour stomach, I'm gonna stop by my mother's house and we'll grab you some homemade soup."

"For real?" She responded in surprise.

"For real, my sweet baby. Now let's bounce."

Claire followed him back to his Benz. All her life she wanted somebody like him to be in love with. Still, she wasn't totally green.

And although Vyce was a dream come true, the baby would give her more love. So she made up in her mind to keep her child, whether he wanted her to or not.

CHAPTER 5

VYCE

The next day in Vyce's Washington DC brown-stone...

"D amn, your lips are so sweet," Vyce told his main sidepiece, 23-year-old Tya, as he went in for another kiss. They were doing their favorite pastime in his bed, fucking. Although Tya was a little older than the women he went after these days, she had other things he needed her for so he kept her around.

His dick throbbed as he poked inside of her, while their tongues danced in each other's mouths. Sweat rolled down his face and onto hers, and the temperature was roasting. Whenever he had sex, he preferred for the heat to be as high as possible, turning the space into a sauna.

"Roll over on all fours," he told her.

Her long brown and gold locs flew over her shoulders as she positioned herself on her hands and knees. It was her birthday, and because she was easy going, and always gave him his space, he wanted her night to be special. He even bought her the *Neverful Louis*

Vuitton bag she wanted, and placed a few thousand inside so that she could buy whatever she desired.

"I want some of that ass now," he warned.

Tya trembled, afraid he'd be as rough as he was on her the last time. When she felt his warm face brush against her ass cheeks, before spit flew in her hole, she relaxed a little. He was loosening it up for her. In anticipation she began to wiggle her hips, and suddenly she welcomed the moment she once dreaded.

"Oh, you want me to get up in that thing don't you? I see you backing that up for me."

She looked at the dresser, at the large brown Louis Vuitton paper bag, which held her purse, and realized he'd been a good boy today. And because of it she would allow him to do whatever he wanted. "I'm all yours, Vyce."

Tya's face twisted as she felt the tip of his stick loitering around her asshole. Her breasts smashed against the damp sheet, as she hiked her ass high into the air.

"Stop fucking around, and fuck me," she demanded wanting to feel the pleasure or pain.

He grinned, because he loved for them to beg, especially when it came to the ass sex. Instead of playing around, he eased into her warm snug hole and pumped her slowly at first.

When her body began to tingle, Tya bit down on her bottom lip a little too hard and could taste the saltiness of her own blood. For some reason, today, anal sex wasn't hurting her like it had in the past and she found that she was enjoying it.

When Vyce heard something resembling a small rock being thrown at the window, at first he tried to ignore it. Besides, sex with Tya was always special which is one of the many reasons he kept her around, and he hated interruptions. It didn't matter how rough he got with her, or what she hadn't done before. For his love she was willing to do it all.

When he heard another sound on his window, re-sembling a larger rock, he pulled out of Tya and said, "Hold up, sweet baby."

When he looked out of the window, he almost stumbled when he saw who was standing outside. There, in his front yard, was Bobbi. The girl he met in KFC, along with a redbone he didn't recognize.

"What the fuck does this bitch want?" He asked himself as he grabbed his navy blue and red Polo robe off of the edge of the chair. He slid it on along with his navy blue slippers.

"Is everything okay?" Tya asked turning over in the bed, covering her breasts with the white sheet. "I can come down there if you got girl trouble."

He smiled at his little soldier. "That's cool, my sweet baby. I got it. You just keep that thing warm, I'll be right back."

When he made it downstairs, he pulled the front door open with an attitude and rushed outside. It didn't dawn on him that he never gave her his address, let alone his full name. "How did you find out where I lived?"

"Don't worry about all that, nigga," Pookie said jumping in front of him. "Why you try and play my cousin by giving her a wrong number? That's some foul ass shit you did, but guess what, we found that ass."

"I don't know what ya'll doing here, but you got to get the fuck up off of my property."

"Fuck your property, bitch," Bobbi responded. "Why you play me like that by leaving me in the ho-tel? Talking about I'm gonna get a wine cooler but never came back. What type of janky shit was that?"

"Look...uh...what's your name again?"

"Ughh, this mothafucka don't even know your name," Pookie interjected. "You should smack the shit out of him. If I were you I would."

"If you hit me you'll never hit another man in your life." He promised. "Now look, I don't know why you showed up at my house but—"

"She showed up at your house because she's preg-nant."

His jaw dropped. This marked the second time in the week someone claimed they were pregnant by him. Now that he thought about it, it all made sense. He had sex with Bobbi and Claire on the same day. If their pussies were the jackpot he would be rich, instead he was about to be a father. Provided she didn't fuck anybody else, the kid could possibly be his, which is why he had to get rid of it.

"You can't have no baby by me. Sorry, shawty."

She placed hands on both of her hips. "I can and I will."

"If you do, I'm not helping you pay for shit for that kid. I'm dead serious."

"He trying to play you again," Pookie yelled. "I say we fuck up his car now, and get this nigga back in line."

Bobbi's eyes sparked after hearing her cousin's suggestion. With time on her hands she said, "I think you're right." Both of them removed switchblades from their jeans and flicked them. "You get the left, and I'll scratch up the right side."

"If either one of you touch my car, I'll kill both of you bitches today! I'm not even fucking around."

"With what"— Bobbi looked him up and down— "your dick?"

Both of the girls moved toward his car. He was going to strangle Bobbi when a gunshot fired in the background. When all three of them looked up at his house they saw a naked girl with long dreads aiming in their direction. Vyce couldn't do anything but smile.

"From this distance I can shoot you"— she pointed the barrel towards Pookie— "and you," she continued aiming at Bobbi. "Unless you get from around here now."

"And who the fuck are you?" Bobbi asked with her hands on her hips, unmoved by the threat on her life.

"That shouldn't be your concern. What you should be thinking about is if I'm serious or not. As well as how good is my accuracy."

Tya had always been on Vyce's favorite list, but what she was doing now made him feel her even more.

"Come on, Bobbi, this nigga not even worth it," Pookie said looking at the gun's eyehole. She was scared to death but she'd never let her cousin know. "We'll see this bitch ass nigga again."

"Yes he is."

"Yes he is what?" Pookie asked.

"Yes he is worth it. He's real worth it." She looked at his fuzzy braids, which were messy due to having sex, and then his eyes. "Since I don't have no job, all I got is a lot of time on my hands to work his nerves, and take some of the money he got in them bank accounts I heard about on the streets. When I'm done I'm gonna drain him dry, just like I did that dick."

They both walked to Pookie's car. Before they pulled off he asked, "Bobbi, how did you get my address?"

"When you went to get the hotel room, I went through your glove compartment and found your address on a bill. I found your bank account statement too." She winked. "Know me, boo. I can be real resourceful when I want to."

CHAPTER 6

CLAIRE

Back at Claire's house...

"**M**ama, I know you said he's playing me, but I think he really cares. Maybe when the baby is born he'll come around," Claire said to her mother who was doing another friend's hair in the kitchen. "I have a feeling my little girl is going to be so beautiful."

"Men like him never come around, baby girl. Hand me that strand of hair."

Claire hopped down off of the bar stool and handed her mother the braiding hair. "Everybody's not the same, ma."

"But men like him are. You know I'm mad at you for having sex with him without a condom. But, at least you roped yourself a rich one. That nigga gonna be paying out his ass when our lawyers get through with him. Trust me, my grandbaby gonna have everything money can buy, courtesy of his or her father. How do you think I got my business and this half a million-dollar home? Your father funded half of this before he got himself locked up for dealing. Trust me, I know his kind."

"Well if we do get anything from him, I want a new house of my own."

"What you want a new house for?" she frowned. "You got everything you need right here. Your own room, your own bathroom and more privacy than a teenager knows what to do with. You won't be able to do nothing more if you left trust me. If I had it as sweet as you, I wouldn't leave here before I turned twenty-one."

"Ma, when I turn eighteen in a month I want my own place. I told you, I always wanted somebody I could take care of." She rubbed her belly. "And I'm gonna have that with my baby in my own house."

Ricky burst into laughter. "You know what, I was mad at first until I realized one important thing."

"What's that?" Claire asked.

"You don't know how to take care of nobody else. You barely know how to take care of yourself. So how the fuck are you going to get a place of your own?"

"I don't know, I guess I'm gonna keep trying."

"Well start by cleaning up your room," Ricky responded, sensing her daughter's seriousness with wanting to leave.

Ricky would never admit it out loud, but outside of loving her daughter too hard, she was also a control freak. She needed to know what she did, and whom she did it with and this often made Claire feel as if she would forever be a child.

Ricky had one other child, a still born son, and she never got over the feeling that had she prayed a little harder, he would've survived. This insecurity was the primary reason she and Claire didn't get along.

Once she was in her room, she threw herself on the bed, and then vomited in her trashcan. That was the only part about being pregnant that she never got use to, unlike some girls, she never knew when her morning sickness would arrive because she didn't get a warning. One minute she'd be looking at TV, and the next minute the feeling would be so great, that she'd throw up in the trashcan.

After cleaning the can with scolding hot water and Pine Sol, she sat on the bed softly and looked around her room. The mere idea of living there forever rubbed her the wrong way, and she was suddenly seeking an out. Out of nowhere something told her to call Vyce, even though she realized her attempt would end in vain.

Sure she lied and told him she went through with the abortion. And yes she lied and told him after the last time they made love, that she would rather have him then some ball of baby. But now she felt differently. She wanted love, real love. And she would do anything she could do to get it, provided she could keep her baby too.

Vyce's phone rang five times and nobody answered. She was about to call again when suddenly her screen lit with his flashing phone number. Her heartbeat so heavily in her chest, she was afraid it would pop out. Trying to calm herself down, she took several breaths. When she was as relaxed as she thought she would get, she decided it was time to face him.

Slowly she picked up the phone and said, "Hello."

"You didn't do it did you?"

She was considering lying again, but decided to come clean. Besides, since he didn't want to be with her, what did she have to lose?

"No, I couldn't go through with it." She looked at her long brown hair, and her face, through the mirror across her bedroom. She didn't look pregnant despite feeling it. "I really tried, but my heart wouldn't let me."

"You want this baby that bad?"

"More than anything, Vyce, and I know you don't know me that well, but I'm going to prove to you that I can be a good mother. You won't ever have to worry about me calling you for something the baby needs, without at least me trying to get it first."

"And why are you willing to do that?"

"Because I know you never wanted this child." She sighed. "It's me who wants this baby girl so badly."

"Boy."

"Huh?"

"You said you want this baby girl so badly and I'm saying it's going to be a boy. I don't make bitches."

Her eyes widened and her feelings were immediately hurt. She was learning that he had the ability to strike her down emotionally. When she envisioned herself taking care of someone, it was always a girl. She never, ever, thought of her caring for a son.

"Okay."

"Where are you now?"

"Home." She leaned back on her bed and looked up at the ceiling. "Why you ask? You gonna come over and beat the baby out of me."

"Naw." He paused. "But look, go put your clothes on."

"You trying to hang out or something?" She questioned not moving. Although she wanted to see him, her stomach was so swirly inside she wouldn't care if he said no.

"Naw, I'm moving you into my house. If you gonna have my kid, I need to see you at all times. To make sure you okay, and shit like that. Now if you can't do that, I'm not gonna be in this kids' life. You gonna have to take my proposal or leave me alone all together."

She popped up so fast; she almost threw herself into the wall ahead of her. "Vyce, I want to be sure I heard you right. Did you say you're moving me into your house?"

"That's exactly what I said. Now give me your address and I'll come scoop you."

"No," she yelled. "I mean...no"— she whispered in a smaller voice— "I'll come to you, where do you live?" He gave her his address. "I'll see you soon,

Vyce. And I promise on everything I love you won't regret this. I'm going to make you so proud."

"Good," he paused, "and Claire, I know I didn't want this before, but this situation will work out for the best. I spent a lot of time going over this in my mind, before deciding to make this move. But you have to trust me, and be down with anything I ask or request of you."

"I am! I promise!"

"That's my sweet baby. I'll see you soon, okay?"

"I'll come the moment I can."

←——————————————————————→

It took Claire until midnight to be able to sneak out of the house with all of her clothes. Her mother would never approve of her living with a man, even if he was the future father of her baby. She decided that she would move in with Vyce and deal with her mother later. Besides, it's not like she wasn't going to be eighteen soon.

She had the last item loaded in her Jeep when Packs walked up to her car. "Where you going?"

"Away," she said with an attitude.

Once she was in the driver's seat he leaned on the door and said, "You never coming back here are you? You really are gone for the rest of my life?"

"We have nothing else to talk about, Packs. You left me and now I have to move on with my life. It's not me who made this relationship over, it was you."

"If that's how you feel, then I curse that baby growing inside of your belly, and you'll never see her alive. Not if I have anything to do with it."

Tears immediately rolled down Claire's eyes. She didn't know which part hurt her worse. The fact that he cursed her growing baby, or the fact that just like her, he perceived it to be a girl. She never told him she was pregnant, so how did he know?

"You don't know how much I hate you right now. Why do you always have to be so hateful and mean?"

Instead of arguing with her, he just grinned and walked down the street towards his house. His words were powerful. He said that to her when she was pregnant before, after getting mad at her, and it worked. Nobody but she and he knew about that child that couldn't survive in her womb, and it was just as well because she never saw it alive.

Crying and driving down the street, she eventually made it to Vyce's house in tact. The moment she opened the door he came out.

"Don't worry about getting your things, I'll bring them inside later on tonight." He walked up to her, hugged her tightly and looked down into her eyes. "You been crying haven't you?"

"Yeah, but I'll be okay."

"I don't want you worrying about anything anymore, Claire. I have your best interest at heart."

He walked her into the house and she was surprised at how beautiful the home was. She never knew a single man to be good when it came to interior decorating. So needless to say she was impressed. With all that said, all she wanted to do was get in his bed, crawl up under him and go to sleep.

Vyce had other ideas. He reached down and handed her something. "I need you to go clean the bathrooms and the kitchen." It was a bucket filled with cleaning supplies. "My house hasn't been cleaned properly in weeks, and that will be your job around here."

"I really want to go to sleep, Vyce," she yawned. "I'm kind of tired. You mind if I do it tomorrow?"

"You heard what I said right? That's rule one in my house. You must always do what I say."

She sighed. If she was going to make this work she was going to have to be more flexible. After all, he was her man now and it was her job to make him happy, and to fulfill his every desire. "Okay." She took the bucket. "Whatever you say."

"That's, my sweet baby." He grabbed his keys from the dresser and walked out the door.

She figured he was about to grab her clothes, but it took twenty minutes for him to come back inside. And when he did she was looking into the eyes of a black girl with short curly auburn colored hair.

"Who is this?" Claire asked, not knowing what was going on.

"Her name is Bobbi, and she's your new roommate."

CHAPTER 7

VYCE

A few days later…

"**D**o you have to spread your toes like that?" Bobbi yelled at Claire, as she eyed her tiny feet. "Every time something happens on TV, you distract me by wiggling your toes and shit. Keep your feet out the way, damn!"

She was sitting on the right of Vyce on the sofa, while Claire was sitting to the left of him.

"If you focus on the movie instead of my feet, you wouldn't have to worry about it." She spread her toes this time so wide, they itched a little. "Damn, you're so fucking annoying."

"Bitch, you're the one who's annoying! Always throwing up, moaning and acting like you the only one pregnant around here. Guess what, chicky, I'm pregnant too but I'm carrying my baby like a man."

Claire laughed hysterically. "I know you might be a little masculine in the face, but in case you haven't realized Mr. Bobbi, men don't carry babies."

"I'm five seconds from kicking your ass, bitch," Bobbi yelled standing up. "I'm warning you not to try me."

"Bring it on, slut," Claire responded, jumping up too.

"Both of you just sit the fuck down!" When they didn't budge he grabbed the remote, cut the TV off and threw it on the floor. "Either you both sit down, or get the fuck out of my house. It's your choice."

They heard him now, and they both took a seat, and folded their arms over their breasts.

"Look, I know this is not a conventional situation, but it's what we got to work with. Still, I can't take this fighting shit no more. Everyday I come home ya'll are fussing with each other. Like that's going to make me kick one of you out and not the other. I got a news flash for you both, if this shit right here don't work"— he points at the floor— "both of you are gone. So either get along or no one wins."

He could tell by their facial expressions that they weren't considering the option that finding the fault in the other would not force him to choose one of them.

"Daddy," Bobbi said rubbing his chest, "I don't understand why she gotta be here. I mean, I know you say we must get along and all, but do you think it will actually work? I mean, think about it, baby. We fight too much."

"I'm willing to try, Vyce," Claire interrupted, rubbing his chest too. "But as you can see, she's not. So how about we focus on each other and work things out the best way we can. And, I promise I will avoid Bobbi and her fighting at all costs."

"You not listening," he said to her. "And neither are you." He looked at Bobbi. This shit ain't open for discussion. Both of you are having my baby and both of you are going to live in this house, together. And when I ask you to do something, I don't give a fuck what it is, I want it done."

Bobbi was so angry it was written all over her pretty face. She hopped up and said, "I'll get dinner started."

Since they moved into his home, both of them naturally gravitated toward certain jobs in the house. Bobbi found out that she enjoyed cooking so she prepared breakfast, lunch and dinner everyday. She even developed the ability to make fresh snacks and desserts, which were always hits. When she was at her house she didn't have access to the state of the art kitchen that Vyce did, so she would've never known how good she was. Even Claire, who hated her emphatically, had to admit that her food was the best she'd ever eaten in her life.

Although Bobbi was a good cook, she was a slob and that's where Claire came in. Bobbi didn't bother cleaning behind herself as she busied with preparing the meals. This did nothing but make Claire feel as if she were her personal slave since tidiness was her job around the house.

Claire did such a good job, that when Vyce dropped his slice of pizza on the hardwood floor, he didn't mind bending down, picking it up and stuffing it inside his mouth. If she wasn't bleaching the kitchen and bathroom counters, she was bleaching the toilets and making beds. Claire had proven to be religious when it came to tidiness.

If only he could get them to get along, everything would be smoother, and the bulk of his troubles would be over.

"Let me go to the bathroom," he said with an attitude. "We'll watch the rest of this movie later."

The moment Vyce got up, there was a light knock at the front door. When Claire looked into the kitchen, Bobbi was angrily slicing and dicing vegetables so she didn't hear the knock. Vyce was already upstairs with the bedroom door closed so he didn't hear anything either. So Claire was left to answer the knock herself.

Irritated with everything, she went to the door to see who was there. On the other side was a pretty girl with long brown and gold dreads hanging down her back.

She looked inside and said, "Is Vyce here?"

"Who are you?" Claire glared.

"Does it matter?" Tya frowned.

"Yes it does, because me and Vyce are together now. So I don't know what little situation ya'll had together in the past, but those days are over. I live here with him now."

A tear rolled down her face and she shook her head. "So that's why he hasn't been returning my calls. Because he moved another female into his house." She shook her head. "After everything I did for that nigga. What a low blow."

Angry Claire shrugged. "I don't know about all that, but you aren't welcome anymore around here, get it?"

"You tell him that he just made himself an enemy, if he doesn't return my call within the next twenty-four hours. Did *you* get that?" She said, before walking off and sliding into the white Lexus that was sitting on the curb.

Claire wondered would Vyce be angry at what she'd done, but she was sure she'd find out soon.

CHAPTER 8

VYCE

Fifteen minutes later in the bedroom...

Claire was riding Vyce's dick while the aromas of the lasagna Bobbi had cooking in the oven, filled the house. With both hands cupping her breasts, he couldn't get over how magnificent her body was, even with her being almost three months pregnant.

Always an over achiever he said, "You know I love you the most right? I hope I can tell you that, without worrying that you'll throw it up in Bobbi's face just to make her mad later. We have to learn to keep our convos private"

Claire's eyes widened and he felt her heart beat under his hand. *I got her.* He thought to himself. *Tell these young bitches anything and they'll believe it.*

While Vyce was in his head Claire was in Heaven. Hearing those words was something she hoped for, especially since he moved Bobbi in.

"Do you mean it, baby?" Claire continued.

"You know I do," he said as he continued to fuck her while looking into her eyes. "Damn, this pussy is good. It seems like it's warmer now that you're pregnant with my son."

At first Claire was only half way fucking him because truthfully her stomach was churning. Besides she only seduced him into the bedroom, to make him remember how much he cared for her, in the event he got mad at how she treated Tya earlier. But now, that she knew where his heart lied, she decided to put her back into it. She never told him Tya even showed up.

"You love me no matter what I do?" she asked him.

"Put it this way, in the living room earlier tonight, even though I said that shit about not choosing between you two"— he gripped at her ass cheeks— "if I had to decide who to put out, it damn sure wouldn't be you. I just said that earlier because I knew it would hurt old girl's feelings. But you, my sweet baby, and I could never see you out on the streets. I can't say the same for Bobbi."

Aw shit...after he said that, Claire started to really feel herself. She whined her young ass on his dick so hard; he could no longer hold his nut. One of the best parts about having pregnant young females under his roof was that he could bust his nut inside of them freely, without fear of them getting pregnant. The damage was already done.

Although the sex was great, Vyce also loved the fact that he could tell young girls anything he wanted and they would believe him. He would never have tried some of the things he said on thirty-eight year old April, who he really loved, and to that day would talk to about life's troubles.

Pushing forty April could fuck, cook, clean and dress her sexy ass off, but she was tired of dealing with his cheating ways, so she left him. It was April who decorated his house, and when she found out he was fucking with Tya, told him to stick it up his stupid ass. No...April would have never been so foolish to believe some of the things that he told her, but Bobbi, Claire and Tya did.

After he shot his evening nut into her body, he kissed her softly on the lips. "Damn, that shit was right." He kissed her again. "You went all out that time didn't you?"

"I tried," she grinned, playing with one of his braids. "I want you to feel good about being with me, Vyce. I'm serious about that."

"But look, because you are my main bitch now, I'm gonna need you to start doing some things that I can only trust you with. Some things we have to keep between me and you."

"Of course, Vyce, anything."

He hopped out of the bed, and re-entered with a stack of papers. He flipped sheet after sheet, without bothering to tell her what it was she was looking at. When he got to the last sheet he said, "Sign your name right here." He reached into the drawer beside the bed and handed her a blue ballpoint pen.

"What's this?"

"It's our life, my sweet baby. Now sign it."

After she scribbled her signature onto the paper, he grabbed her driver's license out of her purse, and made copies using the machine in his room. Claire sat there with a dripping wet pussy wondering what was going on. She was too afraid to question him, especially after saying she would do anything for him.

When he was done, he jumped in his jeans and locked the documents in the safe inside of the room.

"Remember what I said, Claire, you gotta keep all things we do away from Bobbi. I never want her to think we making moves behind her back, because it would hurt her feelings."

She rubbed her hands over his braids, which were damp from the fuck session they just had. "I want to be everything to you, Vyce, everything you need me to be, so you can trust me."

Claire had no idea what kind of pain a man like Vyce could inflict on her mind, heart and body, but she was down for the ride.

"Good, because I always knew you were the calm one. The most level headed out of you two. I mean, did you see how ignorant she was in the living room just now?"

"I know right," Claire said excitedly, because he was willing to gossip. "I was the one who was all willing to make things work and she was all like, no. I mean I can't stand her sometimes, Vyce. Maybe we should get rid of her now. I mean, why wait?"

"Between me and you that's the plan. But, we have to move slowly. I want to make sure my baby is good because I don't trust her as a mother like I trust you. It's the only reason I moved her in to begin with."

"But you had sex with her too."

"I have to, my sweet baby. If I don't, she'll make our lives a living hell while she's living here. For real I call it charity fucking. Just let me see to it that this chick has this baby, and I'll think of another plan and we can start our family."

"You promise?"

"On my heart, Claire." He rushed over to the dresser and pulled out a red box. When he flipped open the lid, a diamond so big presented itself that it scared the hell out of Claire. She had never, in all of her young life, seen anything so spectacular. "This is the engagement ring that I'm going to give you, when the time is right."

Claire fanned her face with her hand because she was so excited that her body temperature rose to staggering levels. "Are you serious, Vyce?"

"I'm dead ass serious. You gonna rock this ring and be Mrs. Vyce Anderson, and niggas gonna know it. But you gotta do whatever I say, when I say it. If you don't I'm not gonna believe you down for me and the cause."

"You won't have no problems with me, Vyce. I don't even give a fuck what I gotta do. Anything you want from me it's done. My heart and body is yours."

Sure the ring would never come anywhere near her finger. And of course the ring belonged to April, before she threw it in his face and told him to stick it up his ass along with the house. Still, Claire didn't need to know that, because it was all about mind games with him.

"That makes me feel so good to hear, my sweet baby, because I need you to be strong through all of this. Anybody who gonna be my wife gotta be hard bodied."

"I will, Vyce. You can count on me."

"Damn, you making me want to fuck your pretty ass again, being all strong and shit. You want me to lick that pussy?"

"Yes," she nodded her head so fast up and down, her chin stabbed several times into her collarbone.

Vyce pushed her back and ate her pussy so good, Claire declared him as her new God. If he wanted, she would give him her soul, and it was exactly what Vyce was aiming for.

After Vyce ate her pussy clean, Claire decided to call her mother. Since she left home she didn't bother telling her where she went, and she figured now was the time, especially since she was about to be Mrs. Vyce Anderson and all. But as usual, her mother broke her down several notches.

"Claire, that man has no intentions on marrying you. And if you believe that he will, you'll be one stupid mothafucka waiting."

"But he is, ma, I saw the ring and everything."

She sat her naked ass on the top of his pillow, on the side where Bobbi slept when they stayed in his room. Although they both had rooms of their own within the house, during the week he allowed them to share his bed, but the weekends belonged to him.

"Girl, you are dumber than I realized and I'm ashamed of your upbringing. It's obvious if he got your mind that ripe, that I didn't raise you correctly."

"Ma, he is going to marry me, and when…"

Her sentence was stopped when she felt a sharp pain in her lower stomach. "No, God," she said to herself. "Please don't do this to me again."

"What's wrong, Claire?" Ricky asked worried. "Are you okay?"

When she got up she saw huge blood clots on the pillow, she felt dizzy. Once again Packs curse came true, and she was loosing another baby.

CHAPTER 9

CLAIRE

Two days later at Claire's mother's house…

"Mommy, I don't understand why I couldn't keep the baby. I did everything I was supposed to. I ate right. I talked to it in my belly, I mean what happened? Why didn't I get to keep it? Why did I have a miscarriage?"

"It's okay, honey," Ricky said rocking her daughter in her arms as they sat on the sofa in the living room. "If you didn't have this baby, it just meant that it wasn't meant to be. Now is not the time. I'm sure when you're old enough, you'll be able to hold a baby full term. Try not to worry."

"But why? Why would God do something like this to me?"

"Claire, you can't always blame God every time things don't go your way. You have to take into consideration your thought process, what you asked for and what you prayed for. I mean, did you ever pray to God to keep this child in your womb?"

"No"— she sniffled— "but what about the mothers who don't believe in God? They get to keep their babies so why couldn't I keep mine?"

"I don't know about all of them, but I do know about you, and if you didn't get to keep this baby, there was a reason, Claire." She rubbed her daughter's back. "Did you at least talk to Vyce about it yet? To see what his thoughts are?"

"No, I don't want to upset him."

"Claire, if you're not having the man's child, the least you can do is tell him. I mean don't you think he'll be upset once he finds out?"

"I can't, ma. You don't understand, just a few days ago he said he was going to propose to me. If he finds out I'm not pregnant, he won't have anything to do with me anymore, and I can't lose him."

Ricky sighed. Unlike her young daughter, she knew the kind of man Vyce was. She was aware of all of the games he played on her mind because she was closer to his age at 38. It was frustrating that although she knew him better, having dealt with men like him before, she knew talking to her was useless. Claire would have to learn for herself.

"Claire, I won't argue with you, at least your back home now, and I'm able to take care of you."

"Back home?" she repeated rubbing her eyes. "I'm not back home."

"I know you're eighteen now, but what do you mean you're not back home? You should be lucky that I allowed you to be gone this long. You're still my daughter."

"I can't stay here, ma. If I do, Bobbi will get him and he'll think I've abandoned him."

"Listen, I allowed you to stay there because I know you're legally an adult, and there ain't a thing I can say to you. But you're not going to keep crying on my shoulders when somebody hurts you, ask for my advice, and then not take it when I give it to you."

"Mommy, I'm sorry, it's just that, you don't know Vyce the way I do." Suddenly her eyes widened as an idea popped into her head. "Maybe I can get pregnant again, and he won't know. Maybe I can have a baby and marry him, before he has a chance to find out that I lost our child."

"I feel so sorry for you, Claire," Ricky said in a low voice.

"I feel sorry for me too," she admitted. "But I love him so much, and I can't lose him."

Ricky sighed. "I have to go to work. One of my braiders called out at my shop and I have to cover for her." She stood up. "I hope you'll be home when I get back, Claire. This is not a hotel. I'm your mother, and I deserve to know what's going on with you at all times. But if you aren't here I'm not chasing you anymore."

When Ricky left, immediately Claire's cell phone rang. Vyce had been calling her hysterically after not hearing from her for days. She decided to answer the phone and deal with him, instead of running.

"Hello?"

71

"Claire, where have you been, man?" Vyce asked excitedly.

"I needed to get away a little while, I'm sorry."

"And you do it like this? Without telling me?"

"I didn't mean to, it's just—"

"How you gonna play me like this? One moment I almost propose to you, and tell you how I feel, and the next moment you leaving our home without saying anything to me, or Bobbi. Are you saying it's over?"

"What...no...of course not!"

"Then come home, I want to make love to you. I want to hold you. I didn't know it until now, but I really miss you, my sweet baby."

"You want to make love tonight?" Just the thought of having sex after a miscarriage caused her body to ache.

"What you think? Do you realize that since you've been gone I haven't fucked anybody? Bobbi has been begging me to take care of her over here and I can't do it. I want to save myself for you."

Her heart was thumping. The doctor told her that women who suffered miscarriages are more susceptible to infections, mainly because the cervix is partially dilated. Sex at this point was out of the question. Since he was so anxious to make love, she reasoned that now was not the time to go home.

"I can't come home right now, Vyce, I'm sorry. My mother is tripping."

"Are you still mine or not?"

"Of course."

"And I'm asking you to come back and you're not?"

"I just...I just..."

"You know what, maybe I got the wrong impression about you, Claire. I thought you were a woman I could see building long term with, and now I'm learning that you're still a child. I can't be with somebody like you. I want you to come get the rest of your things tomorrow."

"Vyce, please don't say that. You don't understand what's going on."

"Then explain to me by coming home."

"Can I come home in a few days? When my mind is right?"

Click.

"Vyce...Vyce, are you there?"

She looked at the phone and saw the screen returned back to its regular state, which indicated he was gone. Her heart rocked. This man showed her a ring, the biggest ring she ever seen in her life, that was sure to be on her finger by this time next year, and now he was gone. All because she couldn't hold a baby properly.

When she called him back he didn't answer. She hung up and called again, still no response. She knew what was going on without even asking, he was probably moving her things out and she would be all alone.

73

There was no way she could deal with this later. She had to do something now.

CHAPTER 10

BOBBI

On the other side of town at Vyce's house…

Vyce was sitting on the sofa with Bobbi on top of him. They just finished fucking and her legs were trembling.

"You know I love you right," Vyce said to her, rubbing her short curly hair backwards. "There's something about you that just does it for me, Bobbi. From the moment I saw your face."

Bobbi dropped her head, and tried to hide her blushing.

"Why do you get like that, whenever I tell you what you mean to me? Or how sexy you are."

"I don't know," she shrugged. "I guess I'm use to men feeling me, and then dumping me. For instance all of this is beautiful, but in the back of my mind, I know you're going to put me out soon."

"Why you comparing me with other dudes?" he frowned. "When all I showed you is how I feel?"

"I'm not trying to. I mean, you're the first one who let me stay in his house, took care of me, and loved me. So that alone makes you different. I don't know…I guess it feels too good to be true. My cousin Pookie says that when—"

"What I tell you 'bout telling me what your stupid ass cousin says?"

"Baby, she's my cousin. Don't talk about her like that."

"I don't give a fuck about that bum bitch! What about that ring I bought you? The one I'm going to give you when I propose? Huh? What about that shit? I bet you Pookie has never in her life seen something so real and I doubt she ever will."

"I know baby, and you know I want nothing more than to be your wife."

"And you will be. The moment I find out what's going on with Claire, and find out if she's going to move out or not, we can talk about me and you. But when we do that, I need to know that you are all mine. And that you'll follow me despite all others, including your cousin. Now if you're too young and immature to realize what I'm saying I'll—"

"Vyce, listen to me"— she grabbed his face and looked into his eyes— "there is nothing in this world I wouldn't do for you. Nothing. And when you make me your wife you gonna see how far I'll go for you. I don't care what people say or how they feel. When it comes to you this shit is real."

"I hear you talking that fly shit."

"I'm serious," she kissed his lips. "Now I know I'm young but I'm mature for my age. I can handle more than you realize."

"You sure 'bout that?"

"Of course I am."

"Get up for a second, my sweet baby."

She eased up and he ran to the bedroom. When he came back he had a stack of papers that were stapled together in his hand. He sat down and pulled paper after paper back until he reached the last one. Using the pen he had in his hand he said, "I need you to sign right here."

"What's this, baby?"

"Just some documents that will help me take care of some things around the house."

She tried to take the entire packet out of his hand to read through them, but he wouldn't release it. "Can I see what I'm signing first?"

"You don't trust me?"

"Yeah, it's just that my cousin said to never sign a contract without reading it. I mean, I just want to see what I'm signing that's all. Why you look so angry at me?"

He snatched the documents out of her hand. "You know what, never mind."

Just as he said that, the door opened. In walked Claire, looking as pretty as ever. She walked up to the sofa and looked down at him. The moment Bobbi smelled her perfume she grew angry. She prayed to

God that she didn't come back and now she saw it was all in vain.

"Vyce, I just want to say I'm sorry about how I acted. I know it was immature, and that you did all you could to make a home for me. If you forgive me, I promise to never carry on in that way again." She looked down at the papers in his lap. "Is that something you need for me to sign?"

"No," Bobbi said snatching the pack of papers out of his hand. "I got it."

Without bothering to read the documents, she signed each place he wanted and gave them back to Vyce.

When she was done Claire asked, "Vyce, can I talk to you in private? I don't want to do it in front of Bobbi."

"Why, whatever you tell him I can hear. It ain't like he's not going to tell me anyway."

"I'm not even trying to argue with you right now. Plus it ain't like you haven't been here with him for the past few days, without me. The least you can do is give me some time to talk to him in private."

"The man doesn't wanna talk to you. I mean look at him."

Claire observed Vyce. "Please, baby, just a few minutes."

"To be honest, there ain't much you can say to me right now, Claire. I'm surprised you're even here, considering how you rolled out."

Claire dropped to her knees and started massaging his feet. "Baby, please don't ignore me. I made a mistake. But the last thing I want to do is not be here for you."

Vyce was trying to pretend that her touch and consistent begging wasn't turning him on, but he couldn't deny what he was feeling inside. Just when he thought it couldn't get any better, she sucked his toes one by one.

"I love you, Vyce," she sucked his little toe. "Please don't do this to me. Please don't break my heart."

"I don't know, Claire"— he looked down at her— "I think it's over between us."

Instead of giving up she ran her tongue down the bottom of his foot. "Please, Vyce, don't leave me." She started to lick his other toe but he stood up.

"I'm done with you. I want you out of here, Claire, I'm dead serious."

"Oh my, God, no!" she crawled on the floor. "Please don't say that. You don't mean it. I'm carrying your baby! Have you forgotten about that?"

He stood up and grabbed Bobbi's hand. "If you staying tonight don't bother coming into the room, because the door will be locked."

Bobbi walked with him toward their room, grinning at Claire the entire time.

Claire remained on her knees with a stupid look on her face and a sweaty taste in her toe sucking mouth.

CHAPTER 11

VYCE

Back at Whiz's house...

"I'm telling you, man, I can't believe you moved both of them into your crib," Whiz said to Vyce while shaking his head. An ice-cold beer sat on the glass table in front of him. "You must be a glutton for punishment." He picked up the drink and downed over half of the bottle.

Vyce, who was watching Claire and Bobbi wade in the swimming pool, sat his beer down and looked at him. "Nigga, you the one who told me if you had it to do all over again, you would move both of your baby mothers into your house. I didn't even have that idea before you put it in my head. I can't believe you saying this shit now. So all that was a lie?"

"Was I smoking a blunt when I said it?" he laughed. "You know how I get when I be off the loud."

Vyce replayed the tapes back in his mind. He remembered his face and how seriously he looked when he told him how he would've moved his daughter's mothers into his house. His eyes were red that day. "I think we did roll something earlier that day. But Noodles and Nooch was here."

"If my babies were here then I definitely had something to smoke," he laughed. "I always hit something before I see their mothers." He shook his head. "You know how they can be when it's my weekend. Giving me a bunch of orders and telling me what my daughters can wear and eat."

"Wait a minute, did you tell them they could move in or not, man?" Vyce asked with an attitude. "Cause right now I'm confused."

"That part was true. But, it was only because they hated each other so much that they wanted to make the other's life a living hell. I figured the entire situation wouldn't last long anyway. It would have never worked." He observed the girls in the pool. "But, you just jumped out there and did the damn thing." He chuckled. "So how is it going? They driving you crazy yet?"

Vyce sighed. "It's interesting to say the least."

"Come on, man, I know it has to be some good parts about the situation. Both of them are sexy as fuck."

"Yeah, there are some good points. Plus the best part is that I know my ultimate plan."

Whiz sat his beer down and rubbed his hands together. With an excited expression he asked, "Do tell, and don't hold nothing back. I knew there was something brewing in your mind over there."

"Well the way I see it, you are right about one thing when you were talking about your kids' mothers, and not being able to get along had you moved them in. Bobbi and Claire living together is not going to end well, man, I can feel it. But when whatever kicks off, I'll be known as the nigga who was trying to do right by both of his kids when the smoke clears. Essentially I'll be labeled a hero."

"I'm not understanding."

"They be at each other's throats everyday, Whiz. I'm talking world war 2013 in my house at all times. It's just a matter of days before one stabs the other or vice versa. So I just sit back and wait for it to happen. I have each of them thinking they are the only one, when I have no intentions of marrying either one of them chicks."

Whiz frowned. "And you cool with that, considering they carrying your babies? It's one thing for them to be beefing, Vyce, but don't forget they pregnant too."

Vyce waved him off. "You sound like a punk over here." He grabbed his beer and took a big gulp.

"But I'm serious. If them girls get into a fight then they can injure themselves or your babies. It's one thing to have them going after each other and not be pregnant, it's a whole nother thing for them to be carrying kids."

"See...I hate this shit right here."

"What shit?" He frowned.

"This is when your white heritage starts creeping out."

"Fuck is that supposed to mean?"

"We been homies for so long that I forget that you Caucasian sometimes. But when you start talking like this you get me scared. I mean what you gonna do, tell them what I said or something?"

"Get the fuck out of here!"

"Then what difference does it make what happens to them bitches over there?" Vyce asked seriously. "I take care of them even though I didn't sign up for none of this shit. Plus I never wanted kids, but they stuck me with them anyway. What about what I want or need? Now I got the responsibility of caring for them too when they're born? I wasn't trying to be no father, man. No offense but that shit is whack. I need to hold on to my paper, and I'm not going to let them have it all."

"Hey, man, I love my kids."

"And I'm not saying you don't, Whiz. I see how you are with your little girls. I'm saying that for me, it's not the move."

"I'm surprised you didn't use your CAT Scan story again," Whiz said bending down to the blue cooler to grab another beer. "To hear you say it, they go for that story all the time."

"I tried but neither one of them were buying it. Technology today has made the young ones more educated. FUCK BILL GATES! I guess they heard that CAT Scans don't make you sterile."

Whiz looked at the pool. "Why does the one with the long curly hair have a shirt on?"

"I don't know," he shrugged, "she always wears a shirt these days. I think getting pregnant makes her conscious about her body or something."

"But she doesn't even look pregnant."

"I know, but that's how the young girls roll. They can hold babies up to six months of pregnancy and still maintain their figures."

Whiz laughed. "You wild as shit, man."

"Like you didn't know that already."

"So what's up with your boy? He still got that shipment of Vicodin coming in? I need some more for my customers."

"You know he's good for it. But I may have to find you another supplier soon. Dude starting to feel himself...talking about he might have to raise the prices one percent due to the risk he runs from getting it straight from the manufacturer. Mothafuckas are always being greedy."

"Exactly, always trying to get over." Whiz paused. "So what's up with Angie and Montana? I know since they got caught you don't have nobody to transport your shipment from here to New York."

"Finding somebody is not the problem. Finding someone I can trust is my dilemma."

"Luther and his crew not still jacking your shipments are they?"

"I haven't heard from them niggas in months. I think they locked up or something. And as long as they leave me the fuck alone I'm good."

"And to think, all this happened because you fucked the man's wife." Whiz shook his head.

"Calm down," Vyce said rolling his eyes. "That was yesterdays news."

"But they got a divorce and everything over that shit."

"Fuck them niggas." Suddenly, as he watched Claire and Bobbi swim, he had an idea. "I think I found the answer to my prayers. I don't even know why I didn't think of this before."

"What?"

"I'll send them to New York"— he nodded toward Claire and Bobbi— "to pick up my shipment."

Whiz leaned back into his chair and put his hand over his head. "Vyce, I'm gonna ask you right now to rethink everything you just said to me."

"You not even trying to realize the beauty of it. All you want to do is knock it down."

"There ain't no beauty in sending two pregnant women from DC to New York with kilos of cocaine in the car. Two women who are pregnant by you and live in your house," he said seriously. "You gotta have some type of morals, Vyce, or else that shit is going to come back and haunt you. I'm begging you right now to rethink everything you just said."

"I can't do that. I think I'm on to something."

"I want you to remember this moment"— he points at the table— "always."

Vyce laughed. "So you saying that just to scare me? If you are try again. I'm a grown man."

"I can tell you got your mind made up, but like I said I want you to remember that I was against it."

"Whiz, think about it for a second. They live with me. I'm already in their head and they listen to everything I say, why shouldn't I use 'em?"

"I said bad idea."

They continued with their conversation, until they heard light splashing in the water. When they looked over to the pool, they saw Bobbi's strained face. They didn't see Claire anywhere.

"What the fuck is up with this bitch?" Vyce asked himself.

The moment Vyce got up, he saw what was going on. Bobbi was holding Claire down between her legs, under water. She was trying to drown her.

Whiz looked at Vyce and shook his head, already predicting the things to come. "Man, I told you it would be a bad idea."

Vyce yanked Bobbi out of the pool and tossed her on the ground. Then he reached in the water and removed Claire. He placed her on the side of the pool and rolled her over. Water spilled out of her mouth and nose, as she fought to catch her breath.

Claire coughed repeatedly trying to clear her lungs. "Are you okay," Whiz asked. "You want me to call the ambulance?"

"Naw, man, she's good," Vyce responded, not wanting to involve the police.

When Claire could finally catch her breath she stood up and pointed at Bobbi who was sitting on the grass. "You're going to wish you didn't do that shit just now. Mark my words." She walked away from the pool and into the house.

"Still think it's a good idea to have both of them living with you?" Whiz asked.

"It's too late to change now. I need both of them."

CHAPTER 12

BOBBI

Under the dark sky in Bobbi's new car...

"Bobbi, I know why you had a beef with the girl, but did you have to try and drown her? What if you would've murdered her?"

"Pookie, I ain't thinking nothing about that bitch."

"I mean don't you feel a little bad for what you almost did?" she sighed.

Bobbi was sitting in front of her house talking on the phone. She hated having private conversations inside, because she felt somebody was bound to be listening, especially Claire.

"She was running her mouth and popping that shit in the pool," she responded playing with the radio in the used white BMW that Vyce bought her for her eighteenth birthday. "So I put her in her place."

"You know that girl's pregnant. That was just wrong."

Bobbi sucked her teeth. "So how was service yesterday?"

"What you talking about, girl?" Pookie asked.

"Bitch, don't play with me! How was Reverend Armstrong yesterday at church because I know you saw him?"

"He fine I guess," she responded in a low voice.

"Exactly, because whenever you start acting all religious and shit, it means you been to church and I am never wrong."

"That ain't the reason why I asked you to consider the fact that the girl is pregnant."

"Pookie, please don't play games because me and you both know that's the only reason. Other than that you be the main one telling me to go after bitches for the simplest of things. Come on now."

"Yeah...well..."

"It's okay, you ain't gotta get in your feelings. You still my favorite cousin."

"I'm your only cousin." She paused. "But look, what did old girl do to get back in Vyce's graces anyway? Didn't you say he put her out for disappearing for a few days that one time?"

"Girl, I don't know what that chick did." She shrugged. "One minute he taking me in the back of his room to fuck my brains out, and telling me it's over for Claire. And the next he telling me that she moving back in the house. Who knows what's on Vyce's mind at any given time."

"Well you just remember what I said. Your goal should be to get as much cheese off of that mothafucka as possible, and bounce. If you ask me the nigga is playing himself real close by having two females living with him. I mean who does that shit but an arrogant ass nigga like Vyce? He thinks he's god."

"I know, girl, but don't even worry 'bout me. I'm good, because he's not the only one who's getting something out of the deal."

Although Bobbi was fronting with her cousin, like she was going to take him for all of his paper, the truth was that her only plan was to win Vyce's heart. In her mind she saw them together forever, with Claire out of the picture of course. If only she could get rid of her. She knew her cousin would never approve of her playing second fiddle, so she kept her thoughts and dreams to herself.

"Well let me get out of this car and go inside the house. I'll holla at you later."

"Bet."

Bobbi got out of the car and opened the door to the house. The moment she strutted inside, she was snatched out of her red sandals by her hair and knocked to the carpet. When she looked up to see who the assailant was, she was staring into Claire's angry face.

Claire held her down to the floor and shook a fist into her face. "I know you didn't think I was going to let shit go down like that did you? Huh, bitch? You thought you could fake drown a bitch?"

"I'm gonna kill you," Bobbi promised, as she could feel her curly hair being snatched from her scalp. "You are mine, before this life is over!"

When Claire started kicking her in the stomach, Bobbi realized how serious things were. It was one thing to punch or scratch her, but Claire seemed to be aiming her anger at her unborn child. The last thing she wanted was something to happen to a baby she prayed for every night.

"Oh my, God, please don't kill my baby, Claire! Please! If you want to do whatever to me you can, just don't hurt my child." She tried to cover her stomach with her hands, but Claire continued to boot her belly.

"You wasn't thinking about my baby, bitch!" she responded as she continued to punch and hit her. "When you tried to drown me at Whiz's! And now all of a sudden you want to ask me for mercy? Well I don't have none for you!"

When Bobbi felt another person kicking her from behind, she looked over her shoulder and saw an older woman resembling Claire. She knew immediately shit was over. It was her mother.

Three minutes later, when blood covered every part of Bobbi's body, Ricky stopped her daughter. "Okay, Claire, it's time to go. You proved your point."

Claire kicked her one more time in the belly for good measure. "No, I hate this bitch, mommy. I don't want to go anywhere until she feels my pain. Until she remembers what she did to me."

"Claire, let's get the fuck out of here." She looked at the door, not knowing when Vyce would be home. "Now you said the girl tried to kill you, but at least you're still alive. She gave you that courtesy. Now I'm not about to commit murder on no child for nothing like this."

"But I hate her, ma, and I want her gone! She needs to pay for what she did to me!"

"Claire, are you saying you want to kill her?"

She didn't respond.

"Its time to come home with me, baby," Ricky said grabbing her daughter's arm. "Remember? Like you promised before I got over here. I didn't come over this nigga's house just to be beating up on your room-mate. I came out here to take you home, after you got your revenge!"

Claire dropped to her knees and grabbed Bobbi by the hair, because she wanted to do more damage. She was totally uncontrollable at the moment, and it seemed as if nothing her mother said could stop her. With Bobbi still in the picture, she saw her relationship with Vyce as over. Her remedy for the situation was to kill her.

"Bobbi, you are going to leave this house," Claire demanded. "Do you hear me? You cannot stay here with me and Vyce anymore. He is mine!"

"Please don't hit my baby anymore," Bobbi sobbed. "Please."

"Claire, let's get the fuck out of here before that nigga comes home," Ricky said again looking at the door.

Claire looked up at her mother. "Ma, I'm not going anywhere. Now if you want to leave go ahead, because I'm not stopping you. This is between me and Bobbi."

"What is wrong with you? Are you this way because of what happened when you were with Packs? If you are, you can't keep blaming people for that situation, Claire. You have to let it go."

"I don't want to talk about it or him, ma," she yelled.

"If I leave here without you, you will never be welcomed in my home again. Is that what you want? Is this nigga really worth it? You see what he's doing to you girls. Do you really want to hurt the one person who is standing in your corner?"

"You said I couldn't come home before but was willing to take me back tonight right? As long as I came with you. The next time won't be any different because you're my mother and you're supposed to help me."

"We'll see about that." Ricky walked out of the door, leaving her daughter alone.

Claire focused back on Bobbi. "You will never be what he wants you to be. Ever! He loves me more than he could ever love you, he told me. So you might as well leave now, Bobbi."

In pain but not broken, Bobbi looked her into the eyes and said, "If you want me gone, then kill me yourself. It's not like you're not almost there. I'm sure my baby is gone too, which is also what you wanted."

Claire looked into her eyes. "You have no idea how close I came to killing you tonight. And if you don't pack your shit up now, I might finish what I started."

CHAPTER 13

CLAIRE

In Vyce's bedroom...

Vyce and Claire are sitting against the head-board in his room. He was rubbing her hair softly, while trying to get her to calm down. Last night things got out of control and she was hysterical, and totally beside herself.

"Claire, it's okay," he said softly. "I know why you did that shit. I mean, she almost tried to drown you in the pool. It's understandable why you went off on her. Trust me, my sweet baby. I'm not mad at you. "

"I appreciate it, but I feel so bad"— she sniffled— "I couldn't get past the anger. It's like something took over my body and I had to hurt her."

"I know, you should've saw my face when I saw how you looked on the side of that pool, when she almost killed you. The entire time I'm thinking if something happens to her, I don't think I'll be able to deal with myself. That bitch went ballistic! You're not just something for me to do, Claire, I love you."

"I love you so much too, Vyce." She looked into his eyes. "You are the reason I do everything. I just wanted to hurt her a little so that she would know how I felt."

"It's not like Bobbi isn't okay. The doctor released her and told her to stay in bed. Her cousin is bringing her home in a little while. She looked worse than what she really was, trust me."

"And the baby?"

"The baby's fine, Claire."

This made her angry. Although Claire wasn't supposed to be having sex so soon, she slept with Vyce the moment the bleeding was undetectable from her miscarriage. She was trying to get him to impregnate her again, but it wasn't working, and she was still without child. And to hear that Bobbi was able to retain her baby rubbed her the wrong way.

"I'm glad that her baby is okay," she lied, "I would not have wanted something like that to happen to an innocent infant."

He rubbed his hand over her stomach and she jumped back, and hopped out of bed. "Why you do that? Did I hurt you or something?"

"Uh...I..."

"Get back in bed," he laughed. "I just want to touch your belly."

"Vyce, its sensitive to me. I don't like when people touch my stomach." She knew if he felt that her stomach was getting flatter instead of bigger, he would know something was up. In her mind she was only there because she was with child.

"Claire, get in this bed." She didn't move. "Now."

The moment she got back in bed, and laid against his chest he rubbed her belly again. "Your stomach is flatter, Claire. You eating right aren't you?"

"Of course," she nodded.

"Well cut back on the morning exercises you told me you were doing. I don't want something happening to our child, all because you're going too hard to keep that body tight."

"I understand," she said in a weak voice.

"Look, I know I don't get you involved in the family business, but now I'm going to have to. Two of my employees went and got themselves into trouble, so I'm going to need your help."

Claire could feel her heart beating inside of her ear. She knew what he did for a living and wanted to stay as far away from it as possible. In her mind the less she knew the more innocent she was. "What you need me to do, baby? If I can help I will." She swallowed.

"You know I wouldn't ask you this if I had another choice right?" He rubbed her hair. "So this is very hard for me."

"Of course, Vyce. I know you wouldn't."

"Good, now a very important client is expecting a shipment to New York tomorrow evening. And I need you and Bobbi to drive it up to him. When you done you just turn back around and call me. I'll take you both out to get something to eat."

97

"Vyce, I...I...don't know about this. I..." her eyes widened.

"What you mean you don't know about this? Don't you want to help the family? So its okay for you to sleep in my bed, eat up my food, wear the clothes I buy you, but you can't help me with the family business? When I never ask you for shit. Is that what you're telling me?"

"I'm not saying that."

"Then what are you saying, Claire?" he roared. "Because all I hear right now are a bunch of fucking excuses!"

Claire sighed, sat up straight and moved a little away from him. She never saw him so violent and wasn't sure if he would strike her. "Vyce, what exactly are we supposed to do? I'm not no dealer."

"And you don't have to be. Just meet the person I tell you at the location I give you. You pop the trunk, he'll grab what's his and that's it. Its simple until you go and make things hard, Claire. The fucked up part is I told Bobbi what I needed her to do in the Hospital and she was all game. But you—"

"I'm sorry," she interrupted. The last thing she needed was to be outdone by Bobbi. "I'm on top of it, honey. You not gonna have no problems from me."

"Are you sure, because you're scaring me now. You making me think I chose down by selecting you to be my wife."

"Positive. You can trust me, Vyce."

"Good, because I was getting scared, my sweet baby. I know you are the most level headed out of the two of you. If I expected anybody to be chicken, it would be her, but she was gangster."

"I'm fine," she smiled weakly. "Really I am."

"That's my future wife. Now get over here. I'm trying to dig into them sugar walls again."

CHAPTER 14

BOBBI

In Bobbi's bedroom…

"**P**ookie, we gonna get that bitch when the time is right, trust me," Bobbi said to her cousin on the cell phone. "Fuck her being in the family way." She was hanging her clothes back up in her closet, and cleaning up her room.

"Well when is the time gonna be right? I know it was wrong that you almost drowned her, but her and her mother jumped you. I don't appreciate that shit! If you didn't have a cast iron for a belly who knows what would have happened?"

"Trust me, not an hour goes by when I don't think about this shit. I'm just smart with it that's all. She's waiting for me to strike now, and the fact that I haven't made a move is killing her."

"Well how much longer are you going to wait?" Pookie sighed.

"We gonna wait until her guard is all the way down."

"You should let me go at her when it's time, Bobbi. You know me and Nessie will put a mask on, catch her at the hairdresser and annihilate that ass. All you gotta do is say the word, cousin. It ain't like you don't have a team. What I really don't want is you to be out there fighting while you're pregnant."

"I know"— she sat on the bed and rubbed her growing stomach— "and I love my team too."

She observed the bruises on her face in the mirror, and her stomach ached from the fight. Luckily the fact that Bobbi was from the hood, and fought virtually everyday of her life before she moved with Vyce, made her a thoroughbred, even while pregnant. "

"Well when you gonna use your team?" she laughed.

"Girl, if you don't calm down. You act like you the one who got fucked up, and shit."

"It feels like it," she paused. "You my cousin, Bobbi. I know we have our shit sometimes but that means a lot to me. I don't want anybody hurting you that's all."

"I know, girl, and stop being so emotional. Trying to make a bitch cry and shit."

"Anyway, have you talked to your mother yet? You know she's been asking about you."

"Talk to my mother about what?" she rolled her eyes. "She told me she washed her hands with me, so I don't have anything else to say to her." She crossed her leg and wiggled her foot.

"You know she went over Red's house looking for you the other day right?"

"For real?" Bobbi was shocked because her mother acted like she was through with her. She moved like she didn't care.

"Yes, Bobbi. I'm serious! You know how parents are. They say shit they don't mean all the time, but you're not supposed to take it to heart. It's been months since she spoke to you. It's time to get over yourself."

"You mean months since I asked her for some money. Or asked her to come home. She wanted me out in the world, so now I am and she needs to let me be."

"She misses you. You only get one mother, Bobbi. I mean I know you over there, and you got a life of your own." She paused. "Even though they tried to kill you."

"Mind your business."

"You know what I mean, Bobbi. But Aunt Felicia is dying without talking to you. Just call her when you get a chance."

It was funny that the topic of her mother came up today. Because when she was beat by Claire, the first person she thought about was her. She didn't want to die without telling her that she loved her. She didn't want to die without being in her arms again. Her life flashed before her eyes and her mother was the first person on her mind, not Vyce. She was starting to feel that maybe it was time to call her after all.

"I'll call her when I feel like it, but not right now. Okay?"

"That's all I can ask I guess."

"You are something else, Pookie, always trying to keep family together and shit, but that's why I love you."

"Tell me something I don't know already."

"Ughh, but you so vain," Bobbi giggled. "You are a hot ass mess!"

"Whatever, what you doing tonight? I was thinking about pulling the grill out while its still warm outside. I'm gonna throw some steaks, hot dogs and hamburgers on the fire. You down?"

"I can't come, I got to make a run for Vyce."

"Bitch, you were just bust in your head a few days ago. And already you running errands for this dude? I mean, is there no mercy over there? What is he running a slave camp?"

"Pookie—"

"Pookie, shit! That nigga almost lost you to his other psychotic girlfriend. I don't even understand why you still in the house."

"Because it ain't for you to understand. It's my life, and you got to let me live it how I see fit. One thing for sure if I'm not supposed to be here, I won't be. And if I say this is the situation for me right now all you can do is respect it, Pookie, like you do every other fucked up thing in my life."

"I guess you right."

"I know I'm right." She paused. "Look, I have to bounce, I'll get up with you later."

"Cool."

She threw her phone in her purse and walked into the rest of the house. She was looking for Claire to find out when she was going to be ready to make the ride up to New York.

Vyce, who was at Whiz's house, called five times already to be sure they were still on schedule. He made it clear that whoever didn't handle business would be dealt with accordingly by him. And Bobbi had all intentions of pointing the finger in Claire's face if she was the cause of them being late.

Bobbi opened the bathroom on the living room floor, and her heart stopped. She couldn't believe what she was seeing. She was watching Claire stuff a tampon up her pussy, when she was supposed to be pregnant. She felt like she hit the jackpot with this news and it was the best thing that happened to her, since she moved in that house.

"Oh my, God," Pookie pointed at her. "Oh my, God! You not pregnant! You lied! I can't believe you lied!" Bobbi backed up.

Claire finished her business and then ran out of the bathroom to meet Bobbi in the hallway. She didn't bother to flush the toilet or wash her bloody hand.

"Bobbi, please, listen to me. I..."

"You not pregnant!" she was disgusted by her bloody fingers. "I can't believe it, you're not pregnant!

104

You been running around here faking like you had morning sickness when all the time you was a lying bitch!"

"Bobbi, let me explain…"

"I know when it happened to," Bobbi continued shaking her head, "it was when you were gone all of those days, and Vyce was calling around for you." A smile spread across her bruised face. "Tell me I'm right! Go ahead, tell me I'm right I gotta hear the words."

"Are you gonna tell, Vyce? Because if you do you'll ruin him!" Claire cried. "Please don't say anything to him."

"Why should I keep your secret, Claire?" she placed her hands on her hips. "Essentially you are the other woman. Not to mention the shit that you and your mother did to my face."

"I know and I'm so sorry about that shit. But it was only because you tried to drown me. I'm begging you not to hurt me like this."

"Like I begged you not to beat the baby out of me. Is that what you want me to do? Show you the same mercy you showed me? If that's the case let me call him right now."

"But you still pregnant."

This did nothing but make Bobbi angrier. Claire was acting as if the reason she was still with child was because she spared her. If she had her way, and Vyce hadn't come home early that night, who knows what she would have done to Bobbi.

"I'm not going to speak on Vyce right now. Let's talk about the agenda for today. As you know we have to take that ride to New York, but I'm sitting in the passenger seat while you do all of the work. I'm gonna listen to the music I want, you gonna get my food when it's time to eat, and you will cater to my every need. Are we clear?"

"Anything you want, Bobbi."

CHAPTER 15

VYCE

Later that day in Whiz's pool...

"You know you hurt my feelings right, Vyce?" Tya said, as her legs straddled his waist inside of the pool. "I mean, why didn't you tell me you moved them in? The least you could've done was give me a head's up. I walked right into that shit when I knocked on the door."

"Because I knew you wouldn't understand." He kissed her wet lips. "And you'd get all emotional without focusing on the plan. You smart as hell, but you too emotional sometimes, my sweet baby. You gotta remember that I'm the man, and sometimes my plan may not be what you want it to be. But always, and I do mean always, my will be done."

"I'm sorry, Vyce, it's just that seeing her at your house, opening your door, when I know how you are, hurt. You don't allow anybody to stay at your house, so in my mind it was serious. But you know I'm stronger than that."

"Then what's the problem?"

"I guess, I just got confused." She shrugged. "I mean, you say you gonna make me your wife, and I just want to see to it that it happens. You know what I'm saying?"

"Of course it's going to happen, my sweet baby. But you gonna have to play the cards how I'm dealing them out. Can you do that? Or are you too busy worried about some teenagers who don't hold a candle to you? If that's who you are just tell me now, and I'll step off."

"Of course I can handle, anything you throw my way. Haven't I proved it?"

"Yes on a business level," he clarified, "but I'm not sure if you willing to do what needs to be done on a relationship level. How do I know I can trust you?"

"Because I'm going to prove it to you." She pressed her pussy against his dick, which was hidden under the water. "You know ain't nobody got your back like me."

He winked. "I know you right." He cleared his throat. "But how are the deals looking for the houses I bought out Maryland? Are they going to be built and ready to move in by the end of this year? I have some possible buyers."

"Of course, but me and the underwriter can get into trouble if they start looking into things, Vyce. You gonna have to work out your financials sooner or later to make things look legit."

"I know, I know, but in the mean time I have you looking over things for me. And that's all I need."

"But what if I lose my job?"

"Tya, how much money did I set aside for you?"

"I can't remember…"

"You have two million dollars in an account on the side." He lied. He had some money set aside but it damn sure wasn't for her. "Remember I told you that. You know I'm taking care of you so don't even worry about it. Even if you lost that job, you still gonna come out shining like a star fucking with me. Don't worry about nothing, baby."

"Are you sure, Vyce?"

"Have I ever did you wrong? Think about it?"

Tya thought about how she came to his house, only to be met by Claire. That night took everything out of her because she cared about him so much, and was willing to put it all on the line to be in his life. Part of her mind said he loved her, and the other part, the smarter part, told her to run while she still could.

"You thinking really long, baby," he said. "Is everything okay?"

"Of course." She nodded.

"Well answer the question, have I ever done you wrong?"

"No, honey, you haven't."

"Good, then all I need you to do is start trusting me. I'll lead you on the right trail I promise."

He was just about to slip his dick inside of her when he heard somebody behind him. "Vyce, what's going on?"

When he turned around he saw Bobbi standing angrily at the poolside. Her arms were crossed over her breasts. And her body trembled as she eyed him with Tya, in the pool. She was the same chick who pointed a gun at her the day she came to tell him she was pregnant.

"What the fuck are you doing here, Bobbi?" Vyce asked.

"I was coming here to talk to you about something!"

"Well what are you doing at my friend's house? When I brought you here it didn't mean that you had an open invitation. You could've called me on the phone."

"Vyce, I just got back from New York! You remember, after doing something you asked me too?" she threw her hands up in the air. "I mean why are you doing me like this?"

"Bobbi, you got five seconds to go home." He turned around and focused on Tya's nervous face. "Relax, everything's cool," he told Tya.

Hearing this, hotheaded Bobbi grabbed Tya by her locs, and pulled her out of the water. It bothered her not that she was pregnant, she was acting like she was without child. In her mind if she took the best of Claire's beat down, she certainly had enough strength left to take care of pool chick.

"Get off of me, bitch." Tya was flailing wild arms and she looked like a fish out of water. "Get off of my dreads."

"Fuck your dreads, you dry cunt! You don't have no business with my man."

By this time Vyce had made it out of the pool. Lifting Bobbi up by her waist he tossed her into one of the navy blue lawn chairs. She fell in one but then rolled over, and the chair toppled over her head. By this time Whiz was out of the house, with a cute dark skin black girl following him. They were watching a movie inside when they heard all of the commotion outside.

"What's going on, man?" Whiz asked Vyce. He looked at Bobbi and then Tya, and knew immediately this was trouble. "Everything cool out here?"

"Everything cool and I'm sorry about this, homie. Apparently one of my dogs don't understand that her place is in the cage."

Bobbi stood up. "That's how you talk to me?" Bobbi asked with her hand over her chest. "Like I don't even matter? Who are you right now, Vyce, because I'm confused?" she rubbed her pregnant belly.

"I told you before about your attitude, and you still don't get it. So maybe you'll understand this. Unlike the situation with Claire, I want you out of my house tonight, Bobbi. You got a fucked up sense of entitlement and I'm not dealing with it anymore."

Bobbi held one hand over her heart, and the other on her belly. She wanted answers from him but more

111

importantly she wanted him to choose her. But it didn't go down like that. "Vyce, this is going too far. You told me you loved me and that you wanted to—"

"You not listening to me. I said I want you gone." He interrupted her in case it came out that he proposed to her, like he had Tya and Claire. "Your temper is too sporadic and I can't stand it anymore. All I ever did was take you in when your peoples wouldn't. Whenever you needed money, didn't I give it to you? When you wanted that car didn't I buy it for you? And this is how you act?"

He's right and I'm so fucking stupid for coming at him like this. He was probably just telling her it was over or something. I have to win him back. Bobbi thought.

Bobbi decided that she must fight so she dropped to her knees. Whiz knowing she was pregnant, immediately rushed over to Bobbi, to help her up.

"No, Whiz, please don't touch me," Bobbi begged him. "Let me talk to Vyce first." Whiz backed away and she focused on Vyce. "Baby, I came in here the wrong way, and I'm sorry. I should've known that if she was here, there was a reason, and you don't have to tell me everything. But please don't throw me out of our home. You all I have left in the world, and I don't have any life outside of yours. I'll do anything to keep you. Just let me try again."

Although Vyce didn't know it, Tya saw that his dick was rock hard. He loved this shit. Having a beautiful young girl give up her soul, to let him control it, was everything to him. The power was making him a monster. In his mind he was God.

"I don't know about this anymore, Bobbi."

"If you can see it in your heart, to give me any kind of chance I'll forever be in your debt, baby. Forever." She folded her hands together like she was praying.

He pretended to think about it long and hard, even though he had the answer already. "I'll take you back on one condition."

"What is it?"

"That Tya here says you can stay in my house."

"What...why me?" Tya questioned, looking at him. She didn't want to be a part of anything so ridiculous.

"Come on, man," Whiz interjected. "This is going too far now."

"I got this, man." He looked back at Tya. "Do you think it is okay to let her back into my home? If you say no, the bitch is out on the street tonight."

Realizing she had her destiny in her hand, Bobbi addressed her directly. "Tya, please forgive me for what I did to you just now." She rubbed her belly. "I'm pregnant and sometimes I do the wrong thing, because I'm emotional. I will never disrespect you like that again. Do you forgive me?

"I guess." She felt so guilty seeing the girl like that.

Vyce looked down at Bobbi. "It's settled." He clapped is hands together. "I'll let you come back, but first you kiss her feet."

"That's not necessary, Vyce," Tya told him. "You can just let her back in the house, I don't care."

"It's necessary to me. She came in here and disrespected a situation she knew nothing about, and I want to teach her a lesson." He looked at Bobbi. "Now get on your hands and knees, I want you to kiss her feet."

Crying, and pregnant, Bobbi crawled over to Tya's toes, which were painted with a white and black Zebra design, and kissed the top of her feet.

"I can't watch this shit," Whiz said as he looked at his date, "Come on, baby." They walked into the house.

"Is that good enough?" Bobbi asked looking up at Vyce.

"No, use your tongue."

Crying harder Bobbi bent down and licked her little toe.

"Is that all," Bobbi asked sobbing.

"It's fine, now get the fuck out of my face, before I remove you from my grace."

CHAPTER 16

BOBBI

Two days later in the kitchen at Vyce's house...

B obbi had been slaving over a stove all day, when Vyce came home and walked into the kitchen. She had a roast in her slow cooker, macaroni and cheese in the oven, and she prepped her best peach cobbler, which was all ready to go. All she was missing was her man, and she prayed every minute that he'd come home, and not throw her out.

If Vyce kicked her out what was she going to do? She couldn't have a baby without the money. She wasn't the maternal type. The truth was, the only reason she agreed to have the baby was because she knew he would take care of her in one way or another. But now she may have possibly fucked it all up.

"Smells good in here," he said walking up behind her.

Bobbi's heart stopped when she heard his voice, because she didn't know he was in the house. She wiped her hands on her apron, and turned around slowly. When he smiled she hugged him tightly, pressing his body against her growing belly. Since their fight, he hadn't been home and it drove her mad.

"Vyce, I'm so happy you're home. Can I get you anything? A beer? A snack? Anything at all?" she rubbed her hand against his dick and he stepped back a little.

"No"— he looked behind him— "where is Claire?"

"I don't know," she frowned. "I heard her on the phone fussing earlier. But I haven't seen her after that."

"What was she fussing about?" he walked over to the slow cooker and lifted the top. The aroma from the meat simmering smacked him in the nose, and his mouth watered. If one thing could be said about Bobbi was that she sure knew how to cook.

"I'm not sure. I'm sure she'll be okay though." Bobbi didn't want to talk about Claire; she wanted all of his attention on her at the moment. "Are we okay now? I mean can we move past what happened at Whiz's pool?"

"Yes."

"What does that mean for you?"

He opened the refrigerator and grabbed a beer. "It means that if you're still in my house, I'm fine with you for now." He popped open the beer. "And it means that I told you all I feel like telling you. Is that good enough? If it's not you can just bounce."

"Yes, baby, yes."

"Are you sure?"

"Yes."

116

She turned around and focused on the stove, to prevent him from seeing her tears. Things felt different and she knew it was over. Before long her vision was so blurry that she had to wipe her eyes with the edge of her apron just to see straight. And that's when she felt his warm kiss on the small of her neck.

"I love you, Bobbi." His deep voice vibrated her eardrum and her entire body trembled. "You love me back?"

She turned around and faced him. Everything she felt about him, all of the admiration, came pouring out as she hugged him tightly. "You don't know how much I love you, baby." She pressed her ear against his heart. "And how much I've cried since you've been gone."

"Everything is okay now, my sweet baby. Stop crying all over that pretty ass face. Daddy's home."

"And I'm so happy about it too."

He separated from her, and looked into her eyes. "But look, I need you to do something for me, okay?"

"Sure, anything."

He walked into the living room, and grabbed a stack of papers that sat next to his keys on the table. With them in his hand he strutted back into the kitchen, flipped to the last page and instructed her where to place her signature. Without any questions, she signed everywhere he wanted.

"That's great baby." He kissed her lips again. "That's one thing down but I have another project for you. You up for it?"

"Of course!"

"Good, because tomorrow I need you to make a drop to New York again."

"Okay, is Claire going with me?" she didn't feel like dealing with her, but she would if he made her. Still, the last thing she wanted was to rock the boat.

"No, I have something else for her to do. Can you handle it? You're going to be on the solo tip on this one."

She was partially relieved. "Of course. I got whatever you need me to do, honey."

"That's, my sweet baby."

CHAPTER 17

BOBBI

In a rental car on I-95 North towards New York...

"Y ou sounding all happy now," Pookie said to Bobbi on the phone. "You must be in love again."

"Girl, whenever shit is good at the house, *I'm* good at the house." She was in a rental car driving on the way down I-95. "He came home last night, we fucked, we talked and stuff is right again. You should've seen the look on his face when he tasted the dinner I made, bitch. I poured my heart into that meal girl."

"And where was your roommate?"

"You would bring up that bitch," she rolled her eyes. "She came home late last night. Vyce wanted her to sleep in the bed with us but she said she wanted to be alone. I guess not talking to her mother is really getting to her. Who knows?"

"When you going to tell Vyce she not pregnant?"

"When the time is right. I don't want him thinking that I'm being petty right now, especially after the little ordeal at the pool. Everything in time you know?"

"So when are we going to get that bitch for what she did to you? I haven't forgotten about that shit,

Bobbi. Even though you over there acting like shit is sweet."

"I'll get her when I'm ready." She approached the tollbooth and made a payment. "And you'll be the first to know. In the mean time go back to church so you won't feel so anxious about being violent. You need another dose of praise God."

"Shut up," she laughed. "You not supposed to be playing with God like that, girl."

"You know I'm dead serious though."

"Whatever," she giggled louder. "Did you hear that Reds got a girlfriend?"

Bobbi's heart dropped and she almost crashed into the car in front of her. Although they were not together, she didn't want him with anybody else either. As far as she was concerned he should be miserable for how he treated her.

"I don't want to talk about that shit, Pookie."

"Done," she said. "Anyway, somebody want's to say hello to you. Hold on."

Before Bobbi could dispute she heard her mother's voice. "Baby, how are you doing?"

She cleared her throat and her heart beat rapidly. For a second she focused on the bumper sticker on the car in front of her. It read, 'HEADING IN THE WRONG DIRECTION? GOD ALLOWS U TURNS'. Something in the message gave her chills.

"Bobbi, are you there?"

"Yes." Sometimes her mother made her nervous and she didn't know how to be or act around her. "And I'm fine, mommy. I'm making it, I guess."

"I hear you're doing good, Bobbi. Pookie told me you have a new car, and that you live in a beautiful home. I'm so happy for you."

"Thank you," she responded dryly.

"Honey, I don't want to keep you long. I guess I want to know when will I be able to see you again? It's been months, and I'm worried about you. All I want to do is lay eyes on you."

"Mommy, you told me I'm not welcome home, remember? All I wanted was your help and you turned your back on me. So I decided to give you your space."

"I know, but that was then, and you know I never wanted it to be final. I just wanted you to do what was best for you. But you're eighteen now, and about to have a baby of your own. I want to be in your life, to be there for you and my grandchild."

"I don't know about that."

"Please just think about it. I'm sure you'll finally be able to see what I went through, and how I felt and why I loved you so hard. Bobbi, at the end of the day you are my child, but I had a dream that things are going to get bad for you."

Bobbi parked her car at the address Vyce had on the paper. She was now in New York City. She was a little early so she decided to be real with her mother, since she had some time to spare.

"Mommy, I will never do what you did to me, to my child. Do you realize the things I had to go through, when you turned your back on me?"

"I had too, Bobbi, you were out of control. There was nothing I could do. You were sleeping with older men, getting all kinds of STD's and I was concerned for your well-being. You were uncontrollable and I decided to try tough love."

"But I'm your daughter, mommy, you had a responsibility to take care of me."

"I can see that there is nothing I can say to you right now. Maybe we'll have a better relationship when your baby is born. Because then you could see my point of view. I just wish I could—"

POW! POW! POW!

"Bobbi! Bobbi, where are you?" Felicia yelled, after hearing gunfire so close around her daughter. "Bobbi, are you okay?"

"M-mommy...I...I been shot..."

In a hospital room three days later...

Bobbi woke up and her room was flooded with roses, and daisies. The first person she wanted to see was Vyce, instead when she looked to her left, at the black recliner; she was staring in Claire's face. The fact that she looked so beautiful wearing her red dress, made her want to throw up.

"What are you doing here?" she opened her eyes and then closed them. "I don't feel like talking to you right now."

"I came to check on you," Claire said softly. "How do you feel?"

"What I feel like is none of your business." She paused. "And if you think I won't tell Vyce you're not pregnant, just because you showed up here, you have another thing coming."

"If you must know I'm not here about all of that," Claire responded. "I just wanted you to know what happened. I've been here everyday since you been shot, and today you finally woke up."

Bobbi turned her head slowly to look at her. Her body ached everywhere. "Well are you going to tell me what happened or what?"

"Somebody Vyce had beef with in the past, I think his name is Luther, robbed and shot you while you were sitting in front of the building. You were on your phone, because they found it bloodied and on the floor, so you didn't see them coming. And when they took it out of the car, your mother was still on the line. She told Vyce she was talking to you the entire time, and he seemed mad."

Her heart rate kicked up. "What did my mother say?"

"She's waiting for you to call her," Claire responded.

"What about the work? Did they get that too?"

"They took the coke, and your purse." When she started crying Claire said, "Try not to cry so hard, you were shot two times in the shoulder, and once in the right arm. The bullet wounds aren't fatal, but they could've been. For real you're lucky to even be alive."

As if she remembered she was pregnant, she quickly touched her swollen stomach. "And my baby?"

"He's fine." Claire appeared to be angry when she said that part.

"What about Vyce? Did he come to the hospital yet?"

"He had you transferred back to DC from New York so you could recoup close to home. Plus he sent the roses." Claire looked at them. "But he said he had a lot to do, and couldn't be hauled up in no hospital. But I didn't want to see you in here by yourself, because I know how it is to feel alone. So I came."

Once again Vyce broke her heart. She was starting to think that there was no way they could be together. "Claire, I want you out of my room. I need to think."

"Why are you still mad at me?"

"Because I know what you're trying to do."

"And what is that, Bobbi? Offer you some company? Is that my only crime?"

"No, your crime is sitting up in my room, and trying to play with my emotions. I'm shot but I'm not dumb. I know what the fuck is up with you. Just so you know there ain't nothing you can do, or say that will make me not tell Vyce about you and your fake ass baby."

"It's not my fault the baby died!"

"I don't know shit about you to confirm or deny that statement. What I do know is that you lied to Vyce and you still lying to him right now. Knowing that the only reason you in the house is because of your situation. I wonder what he'll do when he finds out you not pregnant."

"Bobbi, I was hoping that we could be cool and—"

"Get out!"

"Bobbi--"

"Get out! Now!"

CHAPTER 18

CLAIRE

In Vyce's living room...

"Vyce, please don't make me go, please." Claire cried. "Is there anything else I can do? Like ride with somebody else? I don't want to go to New York alone. I'm use to having somebody with me."

Claire was hysterical after Vyce told her that she would have to go back and finish what Bobbi couldn't, due to being in the hospital. Although the original shipment was lost, his clients in New York were not going to continue to show their sympathy for his current situation. They wanted what they paid for and they wanted it now.

"I'm telling you what the fuck you gotta do," he yelled, looking over at her, as she sat next to him on the sofa. "Aren't you listening to me?"

"But what if someone shoots me like they did Bobbi? I don't want to be shot, Vyce. What about the baby I'm carrying?"

"Fuck," he yelled stomping his foot, as he paced the living room floor. "This shit is important! I can't be sitting up in here trying to convince you of something you should be doing anyway!"

"Baby"— Claire sniffled— "maybe Whiz can go with you instead. I mean, maybe if you guys go together, nobody will bother you. I'm just a woman, and nobody will respect me. Plus I'm scared."

Vyce slapped her so hard she dropped to the floor, and scraped her knees on the carpet. When she was down he grabbed her by the hair and pulled her toward the sofa again where he took a seat, while she remained on her knees. "I need you to go to New York, and you're going. Do you understand me?"

"Baby, please—"

He slapped her again, silencing her immediately. "I need you to go to New York, and you're going, am I understood?"

"Yes," she wept.

"And when you get down there, you are not to talk to anybody but the person you are supposed to meet." He released her hair. "You are to check your mirror; to be sure nobody is watching you and you are to be paying attention. Am I understood, Claire?"

"Yes," she nodded holding her face.

"Good, now go clean yourself up and get on the road. I have a rental truck that's packed with the work in the trunk already. So all you have to do is drive to the destination on the GPS. Do you understand that too?"

"Yes," she responded, as she shivered.

"Good, now it's time to get down to business. And, Claire, don't make me hurt you for fucking this job up."

"I won't."

←————————————————————————→

Claire rode the truck slowly down I-95, on the way to New York...alone. She drove so slowly that people behind her kept honking their horns. The right side of her brain was worrying about the cops but the other side was afraid of robbers. She was so nervous that she pulled over to the side of the road to catch her breath. She was on the verge of having a panic attack.

"Why is this happening to me?" she said, looking out onto the road. "Please, God. Help me." Although she had a truck full of cocaine, she was more relaxed, than she was when she first started driving.

Suddenly, she had a plan. She wiped the tears off of her face and pulled back into traffic. But instead of driving in the direction she was supposed to, she took a U-turn. After driving an hour away from the destination, she stopped at a secluded bridge with a small body of water in Maryland. She got out of the rental truck, and removed the duffle bags full of cocaine. Then she walked into the woods, some ways up, next to a field of trees and stashed the bags there.

When she was done, she walked back toward the rental and grabbed her cell phone. "Ma, it's me, Claire. I need your help."

"What do you want?" She paused. "Because you can't come back home, Claire. I'm tired of being used and abused by you. The only thing you care about is yourself, so the only thing I care about is myself too."

"I know, ma, and I'm not trying to come home. I understand that I burned that bridge."

"So what do you want then?"

"Do you think that you can come get me? If you could I'd really appreciate it. I'm stranded, with no where to go." When her mother didn't respond she grew more desperate. "Please, mommy."

"I guess a ride doesn't hurt."

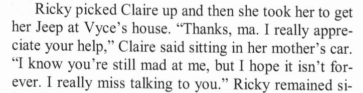

Ricky picked Claire up and then she took her to get her Jeep at Vyce's house. "Thanks, ma. I really appreciate your help," Claire said sitting in her mother's car. "I know you're still mad at me, but I hope it isn't forever. I really miss talking to you." Ricky remained silent. "Ma, are you gonna say anything?"

"I have nothing else to say, because I said my peace already. Now please get out, I have a client in an hour."

Claire slid out of her mother's car, and watched her pull off. She forced her tears back because she had work to do. Claire drove her Jeep to the place where the rental was parked and pulled behind it. Then she got back into the rental, turned it on, left it in drive and jumped back into her Jeep. Then she tapped the truck several times from behind until it rolled into the water.

She waited until water covered the entire top of the rental car. When she was done, she parked her Jeep some ways away from the scene, and jumped into the water to get wet. When she was done setting up her plot, she called Vyce to tell him that she had been in an accident.

"Baby, please don't be mad at me, but I've been in a car accident."

"Where are you now?" he asked with an attitude.

She gave him the address.

Instead of asking how she was doing, he said, "What happened to the package?"

"Baby, did you hear me," she sniffled. "I was in an accident because somebody hit me from behind. The rental fell into the water and I couldn't get it."

"I'm on my way, Claire. Don't move."

CHAPTER 19

VYCE

In Vyce's bedroom...

Vyce beat Claire unmercifully in the bedroom of his house. Although she tried to
tell him that she'd been in a car accident,
he didn't believe a word she said. Essentially the
young dumb girl made a move and thought she could
get over, but he was smarter than her.

"You think I'm a fool," he hit her again in the face.
"You think I was born yesterday?" he looked down at
her. "And that you can run some kind of game on me?
Don't you know I'm smarter than you, bitch?" He
kicked her in the stomach. "Don't you?"

"Vyce," she said in a weak voice, "please, you're
hurting me." It felt like her ribs were crashing in on
her. "I can't breathe."

"You think I give a fuck about your breaths? I'm a
wanted man, because of that shit you pulled today!" he
looked down on her with clenched fists. "Them niggas
are on they're way up here to see about me, and it's all
your fault! You think I care about you lying down on
the floor crying? Do you? You had one job, Claire!

Just one! Transfer the package, and still you couldn't do it."

"I didn't mean to get into the car accident, Vyce" she lied. "It wasn't my fault. Somebody was texting and ran into me. And instead of stopping he ran away from the scene of the crime."

"Then why was your Jeep up there? Huh? Didn't you think that I would see it, as I came to pick you up?"

"My Jeep was there because after I called you, I called my mother to drop off my car. I didn't know how long you would be."

"You ain't nothing but a lying ass slut. You lucky I found that work you tried to stash, stupid ass bitch." He hit her again in the stomach. "And anybody as dumb as you, will not have my baby." He struck her again.

"Vyce, please, don't hurt me anymore. I…I can't take it."

Just when he was about to hit her again, Bobbi entered the room. She was walking on crutches, and she observed the blood everywhere. Vyce really did a number on her. It looked like a crime scene.

"What's going on? I called for someone to come get me from the hospital, but nobody came. Is everything okay?"

"You know what, there are going to be some changes around here." He grabbed his keys and wallet off of the table. "Some changes that you all better get use to. I'm not going to be taking care of no dumb ass bitches no more, and that's on the real."

He walked toward the door. "Where are you go-ing?" Bobbi asked him.

"To drop off the package that apparently you two were too stupid to deliver."

CHAPTER 20

BOBBI

The next day in Bobbi's bedroom…

Last night scared Bobbi to death. She'd never seen a man filled with so much rage in all of her young life. Secretly she began to pack her clothes behind his back, but she kept them within the closet of her private room, in the hopes that he wouldn't see them.

She took a moment to examine her body in the mirror on the door. It was altered. Different from what it was when she first moved into Vyce's home. She had light bruises and bullet wounds which would forever be embedded into her flesh, and it was time for something to change. Her body reminded her that the man she chose didn't choose her.

When her phone rang she picked it up and saw it was her cousin. "What's up, Pookie, I'm on my way out the door right now."

"Well hurry up! Deep is over here right now and he wants to talk to you about your situation. You gotta come on. I don't want these big mothafuckas sitting in my face all day."

"I'm in route now!"

⟵─────────────────────────────⟶

Bobbi made it to Pookie's house an hour later. Deep and his friends were standing in the kitchen drinking beers, while Pookie and Bobbi sat at the table.

"Okay so give it to me straight again," Deep said. "What you want done and how?"

"I want my boyfriend set up and robbed." She leaned her crutches against the table. "And I need this shit done like yesterday."

Deep looked at his friends. "That's big talk coming from such a little girl. You not gonna be the type of chick who sets up a robbery, but then tell her nigga who did it to save her own ass are you?" He looked at her bruised face and the crutches. He figured immediately she was a battered woman, and formed an opinion about how she was made. "Because once we do this shit, there's no turning back."

Angry, Pookie stood up and slapped Deep so hard in the face; he went into the refrigerator to grab a bottle of water. "Listen, nigga, I don't know who you fucked with in the past, but this is my cousin and she's a real bitch." She pointed at Bobbi. "What the fuck she look like snitching on you or anybody else, for that matter? The women in my family ain't built like that."

"Didn't mean it like that, Pook. You know that."

Bobbi put her hand up to calm Pookie down. "Deep, let me explain to you why I'm doing this. My

135

nigga has done everything to me. I was shot making a delivery for him, and almost lost my baby in the process. I was lied to and a whole lot of other shit that I don't have time to explain to you or nobody else right now. But it's time he paid for what he's done, and I want him to pay in full."

Deep nodded his head. "Okay, so what kind of money is he sitting on at any given time?"

"He'll probably have a few thousand in his safe. But he also keeps money in the basement, but the door is always locked. I want it kicked in. It's not no major lock so it's good. You do that and you'll find at least five hundred thousand downstairs."

Deep looked at his friends again and they all smiled.

"I want 60 percent," she told him.

His eyes widened and he leaned forward. "That's a little steep isn't it?"

"That's my price. Take it or leave it."

"I guess we don't have a choice," Deep replied.

"And you not going to be there right?" Pookie asked Bobbi, more like a demand.

"What are you talking about?" Deep asked.

"I'm asking if she's going to be there because I don't want my cousin hurt." She looked at Deep. "I didn't stutter."

"She has to be there," he replied.

"He's right, Pookie, I gotta be there. If I'm not Vyce is going to suspect that I was in on it." She told her seriously. "I'll be fine, trust me."

"He may think that bitch did it," she responded. "You not the only one living there you know?"

"I know, but I'm talking about me. I have to be there so that he can know I'm innocent. Try not to worry, before you jinx me. Everything is going down smooth."

"You know if you at the house, I'ma have to leave you something hot."

"I know," she said softly. "Just don't hit the baby." She rubbed her belly.

"Oh no! Oh fuck no!" Pookie jumped up. "Ya'll not gonna be shooting at my cousin and shit. It's one thing to give her a few bruises; because it's obvious she can handle that. But ya'll talking about shooting her? Are you serious."

"Pook, calm down, I'm a surgeon when it comes to the bullet," Deep said. "Trust me, I won't hit her with nothing fatal. I've done this shit plenty of times."

Bobbi didn't know is she should fear him or feel comfortable due to that comment.

Pookie sat down and looked at Bobbi. She grabbed her cousin's hand. "Listen, you can't be there. Please. If you stay I'm worried that something will happen to you or the baby. So I'm asking you not to be there, Bobbi. Please."

Bobbi touched her face. "I know you're scared for me, but trust me, I feel good about this."

Pookie started crying. "If something happens to you, I'll die. Please come out of this on top."

"I will," she said. "I promise, plus you already know how I roll."

"When do you want this to go down?" Deep asked.

"Well he has this big real estate deal going down in Texas. I think he'll be gone for about a week. Maybe you should do it then."

"What day?" He continued.

"In a week. But I'll call Pookie to give her the exact details."

"What about that chick your cousin was telling us about?" Deep continued. "The one who lives with you?"

"What about her?"

"You want us to kill her?"

"No, but beat her unmercifully."

CHAPTER 21

CLAIRE

In Claire's mother's kitchen...

"I don't know why men are the way that they are," Ricky said, as she placed peroxide carefully under her daughter's eye. The condition of her face enraged her, but she kept her senses. Claire made a decision to roll in the bed with dogs, so she had to let her be. "They can lift you to the highest mountain, but then bring you all the way down at the same time. At the end of the day it depends on how you want to feel, and how much you can take."

Claire cried softly, and her mother wiped her tears along the way as she cleaned her wounds. "I don't understand why he had to be so mean. I clean the house. I make love—"

"Claire, I don't want to hear that part."

"I'm sorry, I just don't understand what got into him, and I need someone I can talk to."

Ricky sighed. "You already know the answer to that question."

She looked into her mother's eyes. "I don't know the answer, mommy, I really don't. I—"

"Allowed him to bring another woman into your home." She put the bloody paper towels on the counter. "Have you forgotten about that? You gave him a pass to do the ultimate. I mean why would he have respect for you, or that other girl?"

"I know how it looks but you don't understand, I thought he was going to get rid of her. That was always in the works. That's always what he told me. I didn't know he was just playing me."

"You knew what you wanted to know, Claire. You saw what you wanted to see and you felt what you wanted to feel. Men don't change over night, so don't act dumb with me, because I know. Every one of them tells us either by their actions or words, how they will treat us. At that time we can either accept it or run. You accepted."

"So you're saying I'm dumb because I let him move in Bobbi?"

"I'm saying you're dumb because you didn't leave when you had a chance. You can't make him do something he has no intentions on doing. You can't make him love you. You can't make him hold you at night, but you can decide if you are going to participate in how he treats you." Ricky walked away and handed her daughter a pack of frozen peas from the freezer. "Put this on your eye. It's swelling up and I want it to go down."

"Thank you," she said softly, holding it over her face. She looked at her mother who was making two cups of hot chocolate, Claire's favorite. "Mommy, can I ask you something?"

"Sure," she said as she opened the refrigerator to get the milk.

"Did daddy ever hit you?" she placed the peas down and waited for an answer.

Ricky stopped moving and placed both of her hands on the counter. "Yes, many, many times." She turned the eye on the stove and placed her red kettle on top of the fire. "That's why I know so much about the topic. When I tell you I know what kind of man Vyce is, its because they all are the same. Abusive men are so alike you can't tell them a part."

"How long did you take his abuse, before you realized it was enough?"

"For as long as I needed to, to learn my lesson I guess." She shrugged. "It took me awhile but after some time, I finally got it."

"I don't understand," Claire replied. "What lesson did you learn from him beating on you?"

"The lesson of pain. Emotional pain is in your life to teach you something. The longer the pain sticks around, the more important it is for you to learn a particular lesson. And unfortunately it took me two years."

"What kind of stuff did he do to you?"

"Shit, everything. Cheated on me, gave me STD's and even Herpes."

Claire's eyes widened. "Mommy, you got Herpes?"

"Yes." She brought over Claire's cup of hot chocolate in a neon pink mug. "And can you imagine the conversation I have to have with men, before we have sex? That's why I haven't been bothered with them lately, because I don't feel like having the conversation anymore."

"Mommy, I'm so sorry."

"Don't be, baby, I'm over it. Besides, it could've been worse." She sipped her hot chocolate. "I'm stronger for my relationship with your father, and I'm stronger for all of my trials."

Claire had a question to ask her mother and she felt it was best to just do it. If she thought about it, she wouldn't ask. "Mommy, can I come home?"

Ricky placed her chocolate down, and walked over to her daughter. "Baby, I can't let you come home." She placed her hand on her beaten face and her heart ached.

"But why?"

"Because if I take you back in, you won't learn the lessons that are yet to come for you." She removed her hand from her cheek.

"But what if he kills me?"

"Not possible," she shook her head. "You're protected. The last time I was at your house, after we did what we did to that girl, I prayed long and hard. I asked for forgiveness in my part of your upbringing and I let it go. In the morning I got the answer I was looking for. I cannot protect you anymore. I have to let you experience life."

"But he doesn't want me there."

Ricky walked over to the dining room table and brought back a newspaper. "Use this to look for a job. You're eighteen now, Claire. And be glad you aren't pregnant. Because although you could have made it with a child, it would have made things more difficult."

"But I don't have any money," Claire replied.

She didn't expect her mother to hold her ground, and not let her back into the house. Part of her was proud and the other part was angry with her for turning her back.

Ricky reached into the drawer in her kitchen and gave her one thousand dollars. "That will be the last time I give you money, unless, I see you are in school and actively trying to better yourself."

Claire smiled. "Can I ask you for one more thing?"

"What is it, child?"

"A hug?"

Ricky hugged her daughter tightly. And Claire felt her mother's tear fall on her arm, but Ricky walked away before her daughter could see her distraught face, she only hoped she was making the right decision. When she left, Claire focused on the paper on the table.

Something stood out so strong that she didn't understand why she didn't see it before. Suddenly things made sense, and she knew she had to get out of there while she still could.

When there was a knock at the back door, Claire walked over and opened it. It was Packs.

"How you doing?" he asked.

"What do you want?" she rolled her eyes.

"To start all over," he said.

"I'm involved."

"You mean with the man who beat you and fucked up your face?" he shook his head. "You're smarter than that, Claire."

"Get out," she yelled at him. "I will never forgive you for saying what you did about my pregnancy."

"But now that you see what kind of person he is, aren't you happy I did? What if you did have a baby by him?"

Claire opened the door. "Get out, Packs, before I put you out."

He walked out slowly. "You can't get rid of me. You'll see me again."

CHAPTER 22

VYCE

(ONE WEEK LATER)

In the living room at Vyce's house…

Claire and Bobbi sat on the sofa, while Vyce stood in front of them reading his rights for staying in his house. As far as they knew he was supposed to be gone to Texas, so neither of them knew why he was still home.

"I'm sure by now, you both know that I am upset with you." He looked at Claire. "And I know you know why."

"Yes, I'm aware," Claire said flatly.

Her response was not as passionate as it had been in the past. She wasn't begging him to forgive her. Or asking him what could she do to rectify the problem. She was just there.

Not getting what he wanted from Claire, he focused his attention on Bobbi. "And you also know how upset I am with you, for being on the phone during the drop off. After I told you to be careful, and stay focused. If you ask me it's your fault you got robbed."

Bobbi bit her bottom lip.

"And the fucked up part about it is, you were mad that nobody came to the hospital to pick you up," he continued. "Well what about me? What about the fact that I was out of a pack? I don't get any consideration and you never even said you were sorry. How am I supposed to feel?"

"I *am* sorry," Bobbi responded. "I'm so sorry I'm pathetic. Will you ever forgive me?"

Vyce caught wind at the sarcasm in her voice too, and felt something was off. "I don't know what's up with the tone in your voice, but Tya is on her way over here. I don't want any shit when she comes. She's my business partner and you might see her around here more often. I'm just letting both of you know."

"Not a problem," Claire responded, waving her hand. "This your world, we just live in it."

Vyce was feeling some kind of way and he couldn't deny his instincts. They were pulling him by the throat, and demanding that he pay attention. *What the fuck is up with you bitches?* He thought.

"I'm glad ya'll sitting over there looking stupid and shit. Because I need both of you to give me a reason to let you stay in my house, because right now I'm not feeling the charity anymore. All you want to do is eat up my food, use my electricity and get on my fucking nerves. I need to hear something good, and I need to hear it right now."

"Vyce, you have been great to me," Claire said. "You took me in when no one else would. You fed me, you made love to me, and I myself, am not worthy to be in your graces. That's all I can say to you and I hope it's enough, because it's all I got."

He frowned. "What is that supposed to mean? Be in my graces? Don't be throwing your big words around on me like I'm some fucking idiot."

Claire tried to save face. "You told me to stay in your graces before." She giggled. "And it means just what I said, my sweet baby," she responded. "If you want me to leave, just say the word and I'm gone. I'm not going to force you to take care of me anymore. I'm good on that right there, please believe me."

Her response caught him off guard and he wasn't expecting it. From the beginning of their relationship she had begged and pleaded with him to be in her life, and now things were different. He was starting to believe that maybe he did go a little too far the other day when he beat her like she was somebody off of the street. Like her crime was to purposely do him wrong, as opposed to loving him.

"So it's like that?"

She shrugged. "How else could it be? This is your home."

He looked at Bobbi. "You feel the same way?"

"I don't know what this bitch over there is on," she responded. "I want to be here and I want to be with you. I love you, Vyce, but if we gonna be together, you have to start respecting me. I can't take the drama no more. Or your unexpected mood swings, and outbursts. You have to show me that you want me."

"And I haven't been good to you?"

"Sometimes. But the fighting, the lies, the hurt, the pain...I want it to stop. I want it to stop today. I'm six months pregnant, Vyce. I can't be emotionally pulled anymore. Do you understand what I'm saying?"

"You two bitches are really feeling yourself aren't you?" he frowned. "You think just cause as nigga beat on your head a little, that you some sort of victim now? Well I'm still not hearing a reason on why I should let you stay in my house."

"I already spoke on that point," Claire responded. "I told you I can leave your house, and give you the freedom you been asking for since I got here. Is that what you want me to do?"

"If I want you to leave than I'll say it."

"So what's the problem then, Vyce," Bobbi questioned. "If she wants to leave, let her. She's been a problem since day one. With her gone, we will finally get what we wanted, a family."

"I think you two need to appreciate the fact that I—"

When the front door kicked in, and three dudes in ski masks burst inside, Vyce lost control of his bowels, and what he was about to say next. When he appeared frozen in the middle of the floor, the largest man cracked him in the center of the back of his head with the butt of his gun.

"You know what time it is," the biggest man said aiming the shotgun at Vyce. "It's a robbery. And I need everybody else on the mothafuckin floor right now too."

Bobbi quickly dropped to the floor and Claire, scared for her life, followed her lead.

"I don't got nothing in here, man," Vyce lied looking up at him. "If somebody told you I was sitting on something, they were selling you shit. I'm telling you, ya'll got the wrong person."

Deep came down so hard on his forehead with the butt of the gun, that Vyce swallowed two of his teeth in the process. As if he didn't see enough blood, he cracked the double barrel shot gun on his cheek, which opened up his face. "You want to play that game again, or you wanna start talking and telling me where the paper at?"

"I got three hundred thousand in the basement," he said with his bloody mouth. "The code is 6893. That's all I got in here, I swear to God, man! I wouldn't even play ya'll like that because I can see you about your business."

"Go open the safe, and I'll keep him company," Deep told one of his men. He looked at the other man. "You open everything that's closed in this mothafucka and see what else you can find. I don't care if you have to tear this bitch up to do it."

While Claire was sobbing uncontrollably, Bobbi was balled over on her side, as silent as a mouse. "Be quiet, bitch," Deep yelled at Claire. "Before I give you something real good that you can feel to whine about."

She tried to press her hands over her mouth, but she was unable to mute her cries. "You think I'm playing, bitch," he asked Claire. "You think it's a fucking joke?"

She removed her hand and said, "No...I...don't think you're a joke. I'm just scared that's all."

"You 'bout to have a reason to be scared in a minute if you don't shut the fuck up."

When Deep's men came back upstairs, they had huge smiles on their faces. "We found the money, and some jewelry. I think this is the big one."

Concluding their work, Deep looked at the hostages on the floor and said, "Unfortunately I wish I could leave you all alive. But as we all know, dead witnesses tell no—"

Like a grasshopper, Vyce hopped up, and pushed Deep into the China cabinet before he could finish his statement. He was able to pull the door open and run for his life. Although Deep was caught off guard, his men let off three rounds in his direction, but it was useless because like a flash Vyce was gone.

"Fuck! I knew I should've burned that mothafucka when I first got inside," Deep said.

"I told you, to let one off in his head but you didn't listen," Goon A responded. "Now look!"

Outraged, but still trying to keep up with the plan, he addressed Claire and Bobbi. "Sorry, ladies, but I can't leave any witnesses. And since it's just a matter of time before he gets the police, I gotta do what we came to do. Hit 'em with something hot, boys."

CHAPTER 23

CLAIRE

ONE WEEK LATER

In a small business office across town…

"Mrs. Lewis, don't be nervous. I'm actually glad you came to see me," Terry Gordon said as she sat across from Claire at her desk. "I know this may all seem like it's a lot, but it's for the best. Trust me."

"Are you sure I mean, I won't get in any type of trouble will I?"

While she waited for an answer, she could feel her phone vibrating in her pocket. When she pulls it out to see who it is, Vyce's name with a message flashed before her.

We need 2 talk.

She doesn't respond.

Claire, we need 2 talk now. Hit be back bitch!

Still Claire refuses to respond and he sends another message.

I know u blame me for leaving. But I want 2 know what's up now? R u moving out or what? Because right now I don't give a fuck anymore.

Claire's face contracted as she reviewed the messages. After he left them to die the way he had, she had even less respect for him, as she did before. What happened to how much he loved her and cared about her? The more time passed the more she was starting to discover that it was all a lie. He was all a lie.

"Are you okay, Claire?"

"Uh…yes," she placed the phone into her pocket. "I'm fine."

"Are you sure? Because you look out of it. We can do this tomorrow if you need a break."

"I'm positive," she smiled weakly. "Let's continue."

"To answer your question from earlier, you won't get into any type of trouble at all, because this isn't your fault. I'm actually glad you came to me, and I realize how brave you must be for even coming. Men like Vyce can get into your head and get you to do all sorts of things. Besides, he could have gotten away with this type of illegal behavior for a long time, had it not been for you. In my opinion you're a hero."

Her mouth felt dry and she tried to smile but it was starting to feel harder to do. "Will he be locked up?"

"Do you really want to know?"

Claire remained silent. Her life was nothing like she thought it would be, when she got up with Vyce. Before she met Vyce she was a young girl, with the dream of taking care of someone who returned her love. And now, she was shot, left for dead and dealing with a drug dealer who was cold and calculated.

When the house was robbed last week, and she was shot in her hand with a small caliber handgun, she realized she needed to make some decisions about what she wanted out of life. So she remembered the newspaper her mother gave her, called one of the numbers that stuck out, and now she was in her office doing what may be considered disloyal to some.

Part of her felt like a snitch, but the other part felt justified in her actions. Vyce had done her wrong, and he had to pay for his wrongdoings. So why did she feel so bad?

"What are we waiting for now?" Claire asked Terry.

"For my partner to come in. She should be here in five minutes, so that we can wrap things up."

CHAPTER 24

VYCE

In a strip club in Washington DC...

Vyce was sitting at the bar, nursing a dirty martini. Although beautiful dancers hung from poles in the center of the stage, as they swayed to the booming music, his mind was on his current state of affairs.

He didn't even want to go. But the entire point of him being at the strip club to begin with was so that he could talk to his friend. But because Whiz was playing the Dating Game with a cute caramel colored girl on the right of him, he had to wait to get at his ear.

"So you do like the show Scandal?" Whiz said to the gorgeous black girl with the shiny black Chinese bob, after just buying her a drink.

"Yes, I like it," she smiled, staring into his blue eyes. "As a matter of fact it's one of my favorite shows." She licked her lips. "What I want to know is, what about me, made you ask me that question."

"I just guessed," he grinned wider.

"You're very attractive," she admitted. "For a white boy anyway."

"Is that right?" he smiled.

155

"That's right."

"Well I appreciate the compliment, beautiful, because you're very sexy too," he continued. "Back to the show Scandal, what do you like most about it?"

She giggled. "I don't think I have a favorite part. But, if you made me pin point something, I appreciate the relationship between the President and Olivia Pope. They seem like they were made for each other. And the sex scenes are off the chain."

"So what do you feel about his wife?"

Vyce groaned a little, indicating that he wanted him to rap his game up, but Whiz paid him no mind. He was in full mack mode.

"I don't think anything about her I guess," she shrugged. "If you ask me, she seems to be for their relationship too. She already know where the president's heart lies."

He chuckled. "Let me ask you something else, Queen, you ever dealt with a white man before?"

"No, but I'm willing to try."

After Whiz got her number he turned around and faced Vyce who was tight faced and irritated. "I can't believe you spent five minutes on a situation that required one second. All you had to do is get her number and wrap it up, but you love being extra and shit."

"What the fuck is wrong with you?" Whiz frowned. "You out here trying to kill my vibe and shit."

"I'm trying to talk to you, and you up here booking bitches. If you was gonna do all that you could've stayed at home, man. That's what the fuck is wrong with me."

"Look, don't take your problems out on me, Vyce. I'm the one who warned you against the whole idea remember? I was the one who said don't move them in and don't let them transport the work to New York. But you didn't listen to me, because you were dead set on having your way. And now look. I hate to throw it in your face, but I gotta be real when I say, I told you so."

"You don't know what the fuck you talking about, Whiz."

"That may be true, but I only know what you told me. So if I don't know what I'm talking about, blame yourself." He picked his drink up and took a long sip.

"I'm serious man," Vyce said tossing back his martini. "I feel like something is going on behind my back. It's fucking with me because I can't put my finger on exactly what it is."

"What do you think is going on?"

"I mean do you think they had something to do with the robbery at my house? I mean are they capable of that shit? Because at first I said no, but before everything went down, they were acting funny. Like they wanted to tell me something but didn't. It was mainly Bobbi."

"I can't call it on the robbery, because I wasn't there. I can only speak on what I saw. Whenever they were around you, I saw them worshipping you. I'm talking about they were willing to lay down their lives for you. As a matter of fact, you remember when you brought them to the pool that day and they said they would die for you? I was surprised at how far they were willing to go to be with you."

"What's your point?"

"My point is this. The only way that one of them, or both of them, would be able to do that type of dirt is if you did them wrong. If you treated them like shit and they got tired of it. So did you?"

"I treated them better than any other nigga they ever dealt with."

"That's not what I'm talking about and you know it."

He waved his friend off. Sometimes the voice of reason enraged him. For once he wanted Whiz to be like, *fuck them bitches*. At the same time his honesty, and unwavering ways was one of the reasons he trusted him with his life. Their friendship wasn't about money, or what Vyce could do for him. Whiz was a real man, through and through and in the day where people were grimy it was refreshing.

"I know you don't agree with how I operated but you have to give me credit. I took care of both of them. Yeah I might've smacked them around a little bit here and there, but it was only because they deserved it. Now I don't feel safe in my own house."

"Then put them out, man."

"I am, but—"

"Wait a minute," Whiz said, spotting something in his eyes. "You didn't fall in love with them did you?"

He leaned back. "What? Fuck no! What I look like falling in love with them bitches? They still wet behind the ears."

"I'm serious," Whiz said after ordering another drink. "Them girls cooked for you, cleaned for you, let you talk to them and treat them any way you wanted. I don't know, man, maybe you developed feelings for them. It's possible."

"Even if that was true, which it ain't, they done with me. They think I punked out because I ran when the house was robbed."

"Well—" Whiz said, giving a look that he possibly agreed with them.

"I ain't about to die for nobody," Vyce interrupted when he saw the look in his friend's eye. "They cool and all but not that cool."

"Well what happened exactly?"

"Claire caught a bullet in her hand and Bobbi got one in her leg. The doctor ended up keeping Bobbi for observation a little longer because he thought that after the beat down Claire gave her, and the bullet wounds she suffered after the drop to New York, and the robbery, that she was being battered."

Whiz shook his head. "That's fucked up, dude. She could've lost the baby."

Vyce sighed, growing frustrated with his romantic ass friend. "Anyway, I don't think I should go to Texas with all this shit going on right now. I got a bad feeling."

"Like what? You don't keep your money in the house anymore. And everything of value the stick up boys got you for right?"

"Yeah, with the exception of a few TV's."

"So why wouldn't you go to Texas, and get your money back up? There's no reason to stay here unless you hoping to make things right with the girls."

"Naw, I just got a feeling that's all."

"Listen, Vyce, there ain't nothing here for you right now, man. Don't let a multi-million dollar deal pass you by when your life can change. If you want, I'll watch after the girls for you while you're handling business in Texas."

"What you mean?"

"I'll keep an eye on them, check the house, and stuff like that. If I see anything out of order, I'll kick you an update. Cool?"

"Are you sure, Whiz?" Vyce said looking at him sideways. "I know how you be with them bitches you be dealing with. They occupy too much of your time for you to take anything serious."

"I said I got you. Just break me off a piece of bread when you settle that multi-million dollar deal," he halfway joked. "Cool?"

"Cool," Vyce said giving him dap.

CHAPTER 25

BOBBI

At a luxury car dealership...

Bobbi was standing in the parking lot of a car dealership, rubbing her pregnant belly, and lusting over a used black Benz E-Class. It was the most beautiful car she'd ever seen in her life, and she had to have it.

"So do you like what you see," a young black dealer asked, giving her a suspicious stare. He was doubtful that she could afford it. "You seem like you're in heaven."

"I love what I see," she said circling the car. "I'm surprised somebody gave something so beautiful up." She shook her head. "Another man's trash is another bitch's treasure."

He laughed. "I know, you'd be surprised the beautiful cars we get around here." He looked around. "Where is your man?"

She frowned. "You looking at her."

He nodded. "I get it, I get it. So are you trying to get a loan, and are you putting down a down payment."

"What's the price?" she asked, never taking her eyes off of what she wanted.

"I assure you it's too much for a pretty young lady like yourself to afford out right. Now if you have good credit and a job, we can probably get you into something less expensive." He pointed at another car, across the lot, that couldn't even hold a candle to her current BMW. "Like the—"

She cut him off with a fan of the money from her purse. "Listen, don't disrespect my intelligence or my style by even looking at another ride when you're talking to me. I know what I want, and you never know who's who, and who's working with what in this world, little nigga. Now take that back where you go and get things started."

"My apologies." He swallowed. "If you give me a second, I'll get the paperwork started." He handed her the keys. "You can get acquainted with your new car and I'll come back and get you when I'm ready."

She snatched the keys from him, and did a little happy dance where she stood. But instead of getting in her new car, she walked toward her old ride, which was parked on the curb.

"It's all mine, baby," she said kissing someone in a gray hoodie. "Can you believe it?"

"I can believe it, and you deserve it too!"

CHAPTER 26

WHIZ

In Whiz's Escalade...

After seeing Bobbi make a huge purchase, Whiz sat in his truck with his jaw hung. He couldn't believe she could be so brazen, just days after Vyce caught a flight to Texas.

There was no doubt in his mind now that she set him up to be robbed, and he felt he had to let his friend know. He was partially torn because he wasn't comfortable with harming pregnant women. But, if Bobbi was involved that meant she was dangerous and his friend was unsafe.

Although he didn't want to, he picked up his cell phone to place the call. It rung once before he finally answered. "Vyce, it's not good, man."

"What you mean?"

Whiz sat back in his seat and put his hand over his forehead. "I just saw Bobbi at this Luxury car dealership. She had some nigga sitting in her BMW and everything. The real kicker is that she just bought a new car. Man, this shit is foul."

He could hear Vyce breathing heavily on the other line. "What the fuck you talking about a new car? I bought one for her birthday already."

"She bought what you got now. Just a little older model."

Vyce was silent.

"You there, man," Whiz asked.

"Yeah."

"What you want me to do?"

"You still got the number to the man?"

"You talking about Italian Nicky?" Whiz asked.

"Yeah, put him on to want needs to be done."

"Are you sure you want to go that far? If you got the slightest feelings for this girl, I don't suggest you kill her man. Hear her out, I mean, maybe she got an explanation for how she came up with all that money."

"I'm positive I want that bitch dead, Whiz. I'm so mad right now I feel like coming back, and killing this chick with my bare hands. If she got money to kick out like that, it means she had something to do with them niggas robbing me, and I know you know that already. I want her done so stop fucking around and contact your boy."

He sighed. "Aight, let me get his number and put him on to what you need done. I'll let you know the moment it's carried out."

He hung up but when his phone rang again, he saw it was the cutie he met at the strip club the other night. He was about to answer it until he felt like he wasn't alone. When he turned around he was looking at gray hoodie, who was sitting in Bobbi's car just moments earlier. A gun was raised and Whiz was shot and killed instantly.

CHAPTER 27

CLAIRE

In Vyce's house...

Claire rushed into the house with Bobbi following her. Both of them were anxious and unsure of their next move.

"What we gonna do now, baby?" Bobbi asked with her arms flying by her sides. "Whiz is dead! And it's just a matter of time before Vyce finds out about everything else we set off."

Claire took her gray hoodie off. "Look, I had to move on that mothafucka. He was going to tell Vyce what was going on. So the moment I spotted him in his truck, I killed him for the both of us. How else could I keep you safe?"

"He's gonna find out about us, Claire," Bobbi said hysterically. "He's gonna find out about us, and he's going to put a hit on our heads."

"I wish you could just trust me, Bobbi," Claire said softly, kissing her on the lips. "I doubt very seriously that he had a chance to say anything to Vyce yet. And even if he did what do we care? Our plan is already in motion. We good to go, all we have to do is step off."

Bobbi ran into the kitchen, to get something to wash away the dry mouth she was experiencing. She opened the refrigerator, while trying desperately to catch her breath at the same time.

Claire walked up behind her and said, "How about you sit down, baby, and take it easy. I'll grab something for you to drink."

"Are you sure about this, Claire?" Bobbi sat on the barstool. "Are you sure we can do this?"

"As long as I have you," she twisted the top of a water bottle and handed it to her. "I know we can do this. Think about everything we've done so far." She closed the refrigerator. "I don't even know why we came back to this nigga's house. If you ask me, we should have kept it moving, and never returned. It ain't like we don't have enough money."

"I still have some things here...and...I..."

"Bobbi, I love you, and I know you don't love me back right now and I'm not asking you to say it. I know it's too soon to get you to feel anything for me, but I'm confident that you will in time. I just want you to know that all of my life, I have wanted something and somebody to love. I didn't know it was going to happen like this, or that I would fall for you, but now that you're in my life I don't want anybody else. But you need to know that I will give my life for you and that baby growing inside of your body. And I wasn't going to let Whiz or anybody else stand in the way. He was calling the nigga Vyce I know it! So I killed his ass."

Bobbi smiled, because Claire had proven to go the limit for her. "What did I do to deserve you?"

"You kept it real with me when all others couldn't."

"Yeah, you mean by fighting you everyday?"

"I mean you gave me the real when Vyce didn't. I know this is an unconventional love, but it's our love."

"What if after some time, I still can't love you like you want, Claire? Are you prepared for that?"

"What do you mean?" she frowned.

"I see you are all the way in this, and I feel something for you, I really do, but what if I can't go all the way?"

"Do you care about me?"

"You know I do."

"Well if you care about me, Bobbi, everything else will come in time. And we don't have to rush anything. Shit, after a few years maybe our families can come to respect our love too, but that's down the line."

Bobbi hopped off of the barstool. The mere idea of involving her people made her dizzy. "I think we should keep what we do a secret at first, Claire." She grabbed her water bottle and took a big gulp.

"What does that mean?" she snatched the bottle out of her hand and sat it on the counter.

"Is it more important to you that everybody knows what we do, or how we do it? I mean you have me, so what else do you want?"

"Of course it's important to be with just you," she touched Bobbi's belly, "and the baby."

"Well that should be the only thing that matters. Let's not complicate things by getting more people caught up in our mix, especially our families."

Claire walked into the living room, and threw her body on the sofa. "You're going to leave me, aren't you?" she looked over at her. "You're going to get everything you want, and then you're going to leave me."

Bobbi walked into the living room and sat next to her. "Claire, why do you act like this sometimes?"

"What are you talking about?"

"You're so moody. I mean you have to keep in mind how everything went down between us. We have to learn to trust each other, and make sure we are honest, before we can take giant leaps. Let's move easy does it instead of rushing things. Rushing things is how we got up with this nigga!"

"I am honest with you," Claire yelled, scaring Bobbi a little. "I've never been more honest with anybody in all of my life."

"I know you are trying to be honest now, but what about in the future? What about if Vyce finds out what we've done? Will you still be down for me then?"

"Haven't I proven it to you already?"

"Yes. Kinda"

"Okay, then what's wrong now?" Claire was on the verge of crying, because Bobbi sounded as if she was backing out. "You're making me nervous that's all, Bobbi. Like seriously."

"Claire, you're making *me* nervous. Look, can't we just get our things and leave? Please."

"I feel like we haven't talked enough about this yet. I feel like there are still some things we need to work out, Bobbi."

Bobbi walked into her room and grabbed the two suitcases that were packed in her bedroom closet. Her body ached where she was shot and she was trying to calm down, but Claire was making things difficult. Claire followed her into her room, still wanting to talk.

"What exactly do we need to work out here that we can't work out in our own home?"

"Are we going to move in our own home together?" Claire questioned. "That's one of the things I want to work out right now. Are you moving with me or not?"

"I said yes, damn!" She threw her cell phone in her purse.

"Are you going to be with me, like we talked about the night we made our decision? In the hospital?"

"I said yes, Claire."

"You promise? I want to hear you say the words. Say you promise and that you'll never take it back, Bobbie."

171

She sighed. "You know what I think?"

"No. That's what I'm trying to find out. What's going on in your mind?"

"I think we got off to a bad start. I think we said some things to each other when we first moved in this house, and did some things to each other that we can't take back, that's fucking up everything. It's hurting our trust."

"I think you're right, Bobbi, and I want to correct that."

"Then focus on the good stuff. I mean, since we decided to be together things have been going smoothly."

"That sounds so easy for you to say. I'm not the one who is leaving you."

"I'm not leaving you, Claire! And it is easy. What you have to do is remember how we got together. If you think anything about that day feels wrong to you, then don't build a life with me. At the end of the day, it's your choice."

CHAPTER 28

VYCE

In Vyce's Benz the next day...

Vyce was devastated when he went to his house when he got off of the plane from Texas, only to see that Claire and Bobbi moved out. He didn't know what he expected, but he was seething with anger. Part of him wanted them to stay, and fight for the relationship, and the other part was relieved. With them in his main house he couldn't do his thing, whatever that was.

When he was in Texas he even thought about doing them right, and starting all over if they could convince him that they had nothing to do with the robbery. But when he realized they didn't care, he couldn't help but feel like a bitch. Although he hated to admit it, Whiz had a point when he said he was probably in love with the girls, but now it was too late.

Before the drama it felt good to come home and smell a clean house, with a cloud of hot food hovering over his head everyday. And he felt good during the weekdays when he came home and had Claire on the right and Bobbi on the left side of him in his bed, keeping him warm at night. He realized now that he was feeling himself and that things got crazy.

Through it all, there was one thing he couldn't get past, and it was the fact that Bobbi possibly had something to do with the robbery. He was confused and torn.

He was on his way to Whiz's house, since he hadn't heard from him, to see if he put Nicky onto the girls. When he didn't answer the phone he figured he was caught up in one of his chocolate honies again, which was usually his story, so he made plans to catch him in the act.

But when he pulled up at Whiz's house and saw Diane and Erica's cars out front, he figured they were dropping the kids off. "Aw shit, I don't feel like dealing with this shit right now," he said to himself.

He parked, got out of the car, and strolled toward the house. The moment he knocked once Diane opened the door. Her eyes were bloodshot red and Vyce's heart rocked before she even opened her mouth, because her beautiful brown face was ashy with tears. And when he looked inside the house, he saw Erica sitting on the sofa with the kids, and she was crying too.

Vyce placed his hand over his heart. "Uh...what...what's going on, Diane? Where's my man? I gotta holla at him right quick." His heart thumped so loudly that he could feel it pulsating inside of his throat.

Instead of answering him, Diane was so grief stricken that she ran deeper into the house, leaving him alone. Slowly Erica walked up to the door and said, "You haven't heard have you?"

"Heard...heard...heard about what?" he felt if he delayed the question that what he knew in his heart would not be true.

"Whiz was murdered the other day, Vyce. I'm sorry you have to hear it like this, but it's the truth."

Vyce stumbled backwards. "What you...I just...I just talked to him. When...when?" The base of Vyce's voice was lost within the confines of his chest, and he couldn't talk anymore.

"He was murdered the other day. In his truck." Erica sobbed uncontrollably. "They think it was robbery because his pockets were emptied. I...I don't know what he was doing over there, but whatever happened caused his life to be over. Nobody from the car dealership, up the block, saw anything either. Vyce, I don't think I can make it without him. Whiz was..."

She couldn't finish her sentence and Vyce wrapped his arms around her and held onto her tightly. As silently as possible, he cried and his tears got lost into the mane of her soft black hair.

He was beside himself, because Whiz wasn't just some dude Vyce met off of the street. He was his confidant, the one who proved to be true blue, and he doubted he would ever find someone as loyal as him again.

"Hi, I'd like to make a withdrawal," Vyce said, sliding the document across the counter of the bank.

"Sure, what's your name, sir?"

"Vyce Anderson," he responded, pushing her his driver's license too. "And can you make it quick, I gotta get out of here. I need a fucking drink or something."

"I'll be as fast as I can." The bank attendant processed his account information, and tried not to look at the customer who had obviously been crying. After a few taps of the keyboard she said, "Wait, I don't show you have access to this account. Do you have another number?"

He frowned. "What the fuck are you talking about? Yes I do have access to this account," he yelled, his mind still with the loss of his friend. "Try it again or something."

The bank attendant reentered the account information but still, she did not see his name on the account.

"I'm sorry, sir, although this account is open, we aren't able to give you any information or money from it." She slid his driver's license and withdrawal slip back to him.

"What the fuck you mean?" he yelled scaring her, and the other customers in the bank. "I been in this bank a million times!"

176

"I'm going to have to ask you to keep your voice down, sir. Now I don't know what's going on—"

"What's going on is that somebody is fucking with my money around here." He pointed a stiff finger into the countertop. "I don't feel like this shit today! I'm serious as a heart attack!"

"Sir, maybe I should get the manager."

"Maybe you should, bitch," he yelled, before rubbing his throbbing temples.

This was quickly turning out to be the worst day of his life. First he lost his girlfriends, then he lost his best friend, and now he was finding out that someone had taken him off of his own banking accounts.

When a white man, with a collection of wrinkles on his face approached, he could already tell it wouldn't end well for him. "Can I help you?" he asked Vyce, carrying a sheet of paper. "I understand that there is a misunderstanding?"

"Fuck yeah there's a misunderstanding! Someone has compromised my account! And I need to know how that's possible!"

"Well, I took the liberty of pulling up the account while I was in back. And it appears that although you had access, the account was always under a Mrs. Claire Lewis' name. Just recently, she has since made some alterations to the account that I am unable to share with you. Now I'm sorry, but if you don't leave, we're going to have to contact the authorities."

Vyce's jaw dropped. Slowly he backed away from the man, because he could feel himself about to do him bodily harm. Embarrassed and angry, he ran out of the bank and jumped into his Benz. He stole his steering wheel so many times his hand ached.

That bitch got me. She actually got me! He thought.

Although he saw both of them moving out, he never once thought Claire would be capable of anything so cold and calculating.

Thinking on his feet, he decided to go to Tya's house. He wanted to make sure that the other things set up in their names were safe and unharmed. Because although he was without five hundred thousand in that account, he had accounts in Bobbi and Tya's names too.

As he drove down the road he realized he made a mistake, by entrusting them with so much of his property. But Vyce was a drug dealer and he didn't feel comfortable having his name on so many accounts. In the event the IRS came a calling, he didn't want his name all over the place, even though he owned the mobile chain Vyce Communications.

The hit with the banking accounts and the money stolen from his house put him at a seven hundred thousand dollar loss, but it wasn't like he couldn't make the paper up. It was the principal of the matter, and the fact that they made a move without him.

When he pulled up in front of Tya's house, his heart rocked when he saw a 'For Sale' sign in her front yard.

"What the fuck is going on?" he yelled to himself. "No, no, no! Please don't' be involved in any of this shit!"

Parked, he pulled out his cell phone and placed a call to her. Tya didn't answer her phone, and he was so angry now he was sweating. *I gotta check my houses.* He said to himself.

Vyce pulled away from her spot and spent the next four hours driving to the three new homes he bought that were in Claire, Bobbi and Tya's names. Each one of them was sold.

Suddenly he felt dizzy. All of his life he placed his major purchases in females names. When he was ready to refurbish and flip them, he would get them to sign the deeds and with Tya's help, who was a real estate agent, he would sell them to a buyer for a higher profit. This was the first time he fucked up. Three dumb bitches ganked him for his paper, and he was furious.

"I don't know where you sluts are," he said to himself, "but you better stay as far away from DC as possible, because if I find you, you're all dead!"

CHAPTER 29

HOW CLAIRE AND BOBBI'S PLAN CAME TOGETHER

*B*obbi was fuming mad as she caught a cab home from the hospital. When she was shot after trying to facilitate a drug deal, she figured Vyce would be there for her when she needed him the most. But just like with everything else when it came to their relationship, he proved that the only person he was worried about was himself.

"My house is right there," she said to the cab driver.

"The one with the Benz out front?"

"Yeah," she frowned. If he was home why hadn't he picked her up from the hospital? Why did she have to take a cab?

Bobbi remembered when Vyce first gave her a ride in the beautiful car. Something about it's presence made her feel powerful and strong. She vowed that when the time was right, that she would get her a car just as beautiful for herself, even though she didn't know how and couldn't afford one.

The cab driver parked and was kind enough to walk her to the door, because the crutches made it dif-

ficult. For his help she tipped him twenty dollars, which she planned to steal back from Vyce later that night for being trifling, and not coming to get her.

The moment she opened the house door with her key, she could hear Claire's screams. She tossed her purse on the table by the door, and walked toward Vyce's bedroom to investigate the situation. She stepped inside just as he was about to hit Claire, who was lying on the floor, again.

Standing on crutches, Bobbi observed Claire's blood which was splattered everywhere in the room. Bobbi was disgusted. Of course she wasn't a Claire fan, but lately Vyce had become a monster and she realized she didn't know him as well as she thought she had. Suddenly she was starting to think that maybe she should get away before he killed her, or she picked something up and killed him instead.

"What's going on?" Bobbi asked Vyce. "I called for someone to come get me from the hospital, but nobody came." She eyed Claire who was weeping, and for some reason, she felt sorry for her. "Is everything okay?"

"You know what, there are going to be some changes around here." Vyce grabbed his keys and wallet off of the table. "Some changes that you all better get use to. I'm not going to be taking care of no dumb ass bitches no more, and that's on the real."

He stomped out of the bedroom door. "Where are you going?" Bobbi asked him.

"To drop off the package that apparently you two were too stupid to deliver."

When he left she looked at Claire, and sat on the edge of the bed. She leaned her crutches against the side of the bed and said; "You know he's going to kill us right? It's just a matter of time before he won't be able to stop himself."

Claire stood up and sat on the other side of the bed. "Tell me something I don't know already." She touched her swollen, bloody lips.

"You came to see me in the hospital, and I never said thank you. I want to say it now."

Claire got up and walked to the bathroom. From where she stood she could still see Bobbi staring at her. "It's cool," she replied in a weak voice. "I know you thought I had ulterior motives but I really didn't. And just so you know, I don't care if you tell him I'm not pregnant anymore. I'm done with him." She wiped the blood off of her face and whenced in pain. "You may be doing me a favor."

"What are you going to do?"

She sighed. "I'm thinking about asking my mother if I can come back home"— she turned the light off in the bathroom, and walked back over to sit on the edge of the bed— "but I'm not sure how that will go down."

"Why you say that?"

"My mother wanted me to leave Vyce, the night I...the night..."

"The night ya'll beat me up," Bobbi responded, trying to force the hate out of her heart that crept up. "I remember her asking you to leave."

"I'm sorry about that shit, Bobbi. I'm telling you from a place where I have nothing to lose or gain by lying to you. So you have to believe me when I say I really feel bad. I was mad with you, plus Vyce got in my head, told me he was going to marry—"

Bobbi whipped her head around. Cutting her off she asked, "Wait, he told you he was going to marry you too?"

Claire nodded. "Why, he said the same thing to you?"

Bobbi's head dropped. "What a lying mothafucka. All these months we spent with him, and he hasn't said word one in honesty. I don't even know why we bothered with him for so long."

"That's why he kept us beefing with each other, so we would never talk. Think about it, black girls beef and not get along all the time. We fed right into his bull shit."

"I feel so dumb."

"Don't feel dumb. The nigga got in our head," Claire responded with an attitude. Her heart hurt too because prior to that day, Vyce's marriage proposal was the only reason she hung around. It was the only thing she had to look forward too. "He really had me wrapped up. He's good."

Bobbi started laughing.

"What's so funny?" Claire asked.

"Wouldn't it be wild if we banned together to get him back? I guarantee you that he'd never see that shit coming."

"What do you mean?"

"We should come up with a plan so devious, that he'll lose out in the end. And, a plan that would put us out on top."

"I'm listening."

"Before we go into the details, have you ever looked at any of the papers that he had us sign?"

"No," Claire said feeling stupid. "I put my signature on so much stuff around here, I might have signed my soul away." Bobbi stood up and hobbled to the safe. She pressed a few buttons and the safe popped open. "Wait, you know the code?"

She grinned. "Sure do."

"He gave it to you?"

"Yeah right," Bobbi laughed. "I made sure that I always fake closed my eyes whenever he went inside. The only code I don't have is the one downstairs, because he never lets us stay down there unless we getting a six pack of cokes from the pantry."

When Bobbi grabbed the papers out, and almost fell, Claire, although in pain herself, quickly ran over to help her out. For a moment they looked into each other's eyes before sitting back on the edge of the bed. The stare meant more to Claire than it did to Bobbi, but there were obvious sparks.

"Okay, these are mortgage papers. When we turned eighteen, he had us sign over a lot of stuff. Now as you can see, based on these deeds, we have houses in our names. I think he paid cash for them and at some point he was going to flip them and sell them for more money."

"But how did he do that?"

"I don't know how, we have to find out though."

Claire looked at the papers with her name on them. "He drew these up, without us even going to closing or anything? How is it possible?"

Bobbi shrugged. "I believe we have some credit cards and banking accounts in our names too. We're going to have to pull our credit reports to find out where they are. And when we do, we can shut them down and take all of our cash out." Bobbi laughed. "On second thought, we'll leave one open and take his name off as having access, so that he can know it was done on purpose."

"I don't even know how to pull my credit report. I never had to before."

"It's okay," Bobbi said touching her leg softly, "I'll show you."

Claire felt electricity shoot through her body again. What was going on between them? "So what's the other part of your plan?"

"If we could get out of here, with about five hundred thousand dollars in cash, would you be willing to endure a little more pain?"

"A lot of pain?"

"I'm going to be honest...it will probably hurt a lot."

Claire looked out into the bedroom. She was about to tell her no until she looked into her eyes. *"At this point, I'm willing to do anything."*

←————————————————————→

Claire was over her mother's house after being beaten by Vyce the night before. She was also thinking about Bobbi's plan to rob him, and she wondered if she could go through with it or not. At first her answer was going to be no, when she asked her if she would be willing to endure pain, until she considered what she thought was brewing between she and Bobbi.

"Mommy, can I come home?" Claire asked Ricky.

"Baby, I can't let you come home." She placed her hand on her beaten face and her heart ached.

"But why?"

"Because if I take you back in, you won't learn the lessons that are yet to come for you."

"But what if he kills me?"

"Not possible," she shook her head. *"You're protected. The last time I was at your house, after we did what we did to that girl, I prayed long and hard. I asked for forgiveness in my part of your upbringing and I let it go. In the morning I got the answer I was*

looking for. I cannot protect you this time. I have to let you experience life."

Claire thought about what it meant to experience life. Maybe that was her mother's way of unconsciously saying that she should pursue a relationship with Bobbi, since that was the way her heart was going at the moment, even though she knew nothing about their secret relationship.

"But he doesn't want me there."

Ricky walked over to the dining room table and brought back a newspaper. "Use this to look for a job. You're eighteen now, Claire. And be glad you aren't pregnant. Because although you could have made it with a child, it would have made things more difficult."

"But I don't have any money," Claire replied.

Ricky reached into the drawer in her kitchen and gave her one thousand dollars. "That will be the last time I give you money, unless, I see you are in school and actively trying to better yourself."

Claire smiled. "Can I ask you for one more thing?"

"What is it, child?"

"A hug?"

Ricky hugged her daughter tightly. Claire felt her mother's tears fall on her arm, but Ricky walked away before her daughter could see her lose control. When she left, Claire focused on the newspaper on the table.

Something stood out so strong that she didn't understand why she didn't see it before. Amongst a bunch of gray words, Tya's face was smiling back at her. She was a real estate agent for a small agency, and Claire immediately knew that she was responsible for the houses being placed in their names.

After Packs showed up and left, she decided to call Bobbi. "Hey, Bobbi, you got a second?"

"I was just thinking about you," she said flirtatiously.

Chills ran up Claire's spine but she tried to hide it. "Oh...uh..."

"You forgot what you wanted to tell me right?" she giggled. "I make you nervous?"

She did but she didn't want her to know. "Actually I was calling to tell you that I found out how Vyce was able to get the houses into our names."

"How?" She asked seriously.

"Tya, the girl who came to the house that I was telling you about last night..."

"And the one who pulled a gun out on me and who I pulled out of the pool," Bobbi responded still salty.

"She's a real estate agent. You think she would be interested in making a change over? To our side?"

Bobbi took a brief moment of silence. "She seemed pretty angry after Vyce humiliated me and made me kiss her feet."

"He did what?" Claire yelled. Although they lived with each other, they never had conversations together until the formation of the pact last night.

"It's cool, girl. That's why I'm taking pleasure in getting his ass back now. All sneaky shit comes to the light."

"Exactly," Claire admitted. "I'm going to reach out to Tya, and see what happens. If she says yes, it'll be cool, but if not we'll push off on our own."

"Do it after he leaves town, in case she says no and tells him about our plan. We want the robbery to go down and don't need her alerting him that we onto his ass."

AFTER THE ROBBERY

Claire and Bobbi were in the hospital once again with gunshot wounds and bruises from the robbery they were a part of. For a while the doctor wasn't try-ing to release them, but he didn't have a choice when they kept saying someone robbed their house and they didn't know who was involved.

Although they were aware that the robbery was go-ing down, they were unaware that Vyce wasn't going out of town. Since Claire couldn't get a hold of Deep to tell him not to come, the robbery took place.

In the hospital, Claire and Bobbi spent a lot of time talking because they shared a room. It was at that time that they figured that they were vibing, and that their bond was closer, than they imagined. But the real surprise didn't come in until a special guest walked through the hospital room's door.

"Before you both go off on me, let me say I'm sorry," Tya said, with her long dreads pulled back into a cute ponytail. "I'm here because I am disgusted at the way he left both of you. I didn't know Vyce could be so weak, and to tell you the truth I'm tired of his fucking ass. If he could do it to you, he'll do it to me, and I think I'm moving out of town."

Bobbi and Claire looked at one another.

"How tired of you really of Vyce?" Claire asked.

"What do you mean?"

"We know you've been putting houses in our name for him." Claire continued. "And we need that to stop."

Tya's head dropped. "I was coming to tell you about the houses myself." She sighed. "That's why I'm here."

"Why the change of heart all of a sudden?" Bobbi asked. "I mean, how do we know you won't stab us in the back? Or that you're not here for him?

"Because I'm here because of what he did to ya'll, and what he'll probably do to me if I stay with him." She stepped further into the room. "I realize that I can no longer support him in anything that he does. So

190

whatever you want me to do, I will do. Vyce has it coming."

"Can you help us sell the houses?"

She smiled. "They are in your names." Her head dropped. "But he's going to kill me if he finds out I helped ya'll."

"Listen, we all played the fool for this nigga," Claire responded. *"And if you are honest with us, and help us through this process, we will make sure that you have enough money to get away for good. To start all over." She looked at Bobbi.*

"You heard my partner," Bobbi agreed. "It's time he realizes he can't play bitches the way he has and think shit will be sweet."

The deal was easy to make because it wasn't like they didn't have the money from Vyce's safe in the basement. And since they also found out about the bank accounts he had in their names, they shut all of those down with the exception of one. If Tya acted right, she stood to make one hundred fifty easy.

"Count me in," Tya said excitedly.

"So what do we have to do to sell our houses?" Claire asked.

"Show up at the real estate agency and meet up with Terry Gordon. I'll tell her about my part in every-thing, and explain to her what needs to be done."

"She didn't know that he was putting houses in our names?" Claire asked.

"No, she was never involved."

"You won't get into trouble will you?" Claire asked seriously.

"No, she'll just be happy that the problem is corrected and that I'm resigning. Especially since she'll earn a fee when we get rid of them. She never liked Vyce anyway."

Claire smiled at the both of them. "Looks like this is the start of something beautiful."

"If we can get away with it."

CHAPTER 30

BOBBI

Outside of Bobbi and Claire's brand new home in Delaware...

Bobbi and Claire stood in their front yard talking to Tya, who had her two-year-old son on her hip. The baby looked so much like Vyce, that it made Bobbi and Claire uncomfortable because she said he wasn't the father. They didn't dare go against what she believed, because they could tell that Vyce convinced her that he was not the father, and that she believed him.

"So what are you going to do now?" Bobbi asked Tya. "You have enough money to start all over with. What are your plans?"

Tya pulled the hood over her son's head. The winter was there with a vengeance, and the breeze was icy. "Well I'll be staying with my aunt in Atlanta." She sighed. "It's not like I have anybody to go home too."

Claire blushed, grabbing onto Bobbi's hand, because she was not alone. Tya was aware of their relationship and commented several times that it was cute.

But Bobbi, who seemed unenthused, snatched away from her.

"You'll find somebody," Claire said as she wrapped the Gucci scarf around Bobbi's neck to be sure she was warm. "Moving to the ATL should be nice, because at least you have family there."

"Trust me girl, I won't be there long." Tya assured them. "The moment my peoples get wind that I'm sitting on money, anybody with a problem will come my way. I'll probably end up moving to Delaware or something too."

"What's the plan in Delaware?" Bobbi asked.

"Well I've been researching some land and decided to have my house built from scratch. It'll be our first home and I'm looking forward to the change." She kissed her baby on the lips.

"I love it when things come together," Claire smiled. "I love it when females make a come up too. I know Vyce is somewhere shitting in his pants right now."

Tya's head dropped. "You're probably right." She looked back at Bobbi and Claire's mansion style home and shook her head. "Anyway the house I'm building ain't nothing like ya'lls crib, but it's a start."

"Everybody gotta start somewhere," Bobbi admitted, rubbing her belly. She was due in two months and couldn't wait to drop the load and get on with her life.

There was an awkward moment of silence, and freshly fallen snow dusted the ground at their feet. "Do you think he will kill us?" Tya asked. "Vyce?"

"No," Claire responded in a low voice.

"How do you know?"

"Because he has to find us first. And if he comes this way, fucking with me or mine, I'm going to put him out of his misery for good."

"Murder is going a little too far, don't you think?"

"It depends on who you're talking to."

Tya sighed, and silently prayed she didn't make a mistake. Just like Bobbi and Claire, at one time she loved Vyce too. But unlike Bobbi and Claire, she had nightmares about the day he would find them and get his revenge. And it kept her from wanting to go to sleep at night.

"Well, let me go," Tya said hugging both of them. "We better get to the airport before the weather gets bad." She dusted the snow off of her son's hood, and she hugged them both and walked off.

"We'll talk to you later," Bobbi said waving at her as she entered her rental car.

When Claire walked behind her, and put her arms around her waist Bobbi moved away. Although Bobbi appreciated the things Claire did for her, like preparing the meals, washing her clothes, and kissing her pussy softly to make her cum, she wasn't with the relation-ship shit. All she wanted was to have this baby and find someone she was really interested in, but Claire was playing her close.

Although the relationship idea was over as far as she was concerned, she knew she needed Claire. After all who else was going to take care of the baby when it was born? Her cousin Pookie had her own life, and she was pissed when she found out they were living together, so she would not be babysitting shit. Without Claire she would be all alone.

Although Bobbi didn't put her cousin onto the final details, she had a plan for Claire because of what she did when she and her mother jumped her. Her plan consisted of making Claire a slave, and that's exactly what she was going to do.

CHAPTER 31

CLAIRE

In Claire and Bobbi's bedroom...

"Bobbi, did I do something wrong outside when we were with Tya?" Claire asked as she watched Bobbi slide under the covers to take a nap. "Because you're acting colder than the weather outside."

"No, Claire," she said rolling her eyes.

"Then why are you being so flaky?" she walked closer to the bed and looked down at her. Claire was wearing an oversized red t-shirt and no pants. "One minute we're having fun, and the next you're acting like I'm bothering you or something."

"I don't know if you realize it or not, because you lost your baby, but I'm still carrying mine! And I don't have no time for this bullshit! This type of stuff can cause me to have a miscarriage too. So would you please back off some and give me some breathing room."

Claire's heart dropped to the floor when Bobbi spit those words of venom. She could feel the tears filling up in her eyes, and she tried to push them away before

197

she could see them. Claire turned to walk out of the room, and she rushed downstairs toward the basement.

Once she was there, she walked to her personal safe, and entered the code. The money stacks inside looked like blurry green blocks, because she was crying so hard. Grabbing pack after pack, she realized she had two hundred thousand dollars left, which was more than enough to get a place of her own.

"I'm sorry, Claire," Bobbi said behind her. "I don't know if you can forgive me for what I said upstairs, but I hope you will at least try."

Claire didn't respond. Instead she placed the money back inside the safe and closed it shut.

"Since you won't talk to me, can you at least tell me what you're going to do?"

"I'm moving out, Bobbi," she said flatly.

"Claire, please don't do that shit. I made a mistake okay? I mean, it was wrong for me to say that shit to you upstairs but the damage has already been done. It's just that sometimes you don't give me enough room to breathe and it makes me angry."

"Well it's a good thing I'm leaving because now you have all of the time in the world. So breathe, bitch."

"But I don't want room to breathe if it means you have to go. I don't want all the time in the world."

Claire turned around and looked at her. "Then what do you want?"

"I want you to be easy with me. I want you to understand that I'll probably never be how you want me to be. And I want you to be okay with it. It's the only way it will work."

"When you say what you want me to be, what exactly are you talking about? No more beating around the bush."

"I'm talking about whatever we're doing. With this relationship. You cool and all but I'm not gay, Claire."

"Then what do you want from me," Claire asked. "Because I'm confused as fuck right now."

"I want you to be okay with taking one day at a time. I want you to be cool with hanging with me and us doing the things that friends do. Can you?"

Claire sat down on the sofa in the basement and looked up at her. "Bobbi, it depends."

"On what?"

"What you did upstairs was cold. I will not be disrespected like that again. And just so you know, I never had a girlfriend either. You're the first female I got involved with, and now I'm feeling like it was a big mistake."

"Well you seem to be having a good time," Bobbi replied.

"I want to be loved, that's all. And I wanted to be with you because of everything we been through. But you not going to treat me like shit, Bobbi. I'm done with that type of life. Do you understand?"

"I do," she said softly.

"Good," Claire smiled. "Because I'm serious. Vyce will be the last person who disrespects me, and if I even think you carrying shit the wrong way I'm gone."

Carefully Bobbi dropped down to her knees and moved Claire's panties to the side. "What are you doing, Bobbi?"

"Don't act like you don't know what's up." She said looking into her eyes.

Slowly, Bobbi ran her tongue over her clitoris until it stood at attention. Claire grabbed Bobbi's head and pulled her toward her mound. She was trying to be as careful as possible, but the girl knew what she was doing. As she got her pussy licked mentally she went back to the time when someone hurt her before...and she wasn't thinking about Vyce.

$\longleftrightarrow$

Two Years Earlier

Claire was in her car on the way to Packs house. Earlier that day he begged her to play hooky from high school. He wanted her to meet him at his house, but she didn't want to miss an important test at school. However the moment she walked into class, and saw she had a substitute teacher in calculus, she made a U-turn and left.

She was singing with the radio in her car, when she finally made it to Packs house. As always she walked behind the back of the house, and let herself inside with the key under the mat. Although she was a few months pregnant, she didn't let him know because she was afraid she would lose him. But since her lower stomach started to swell, she decided that today would be the day she'd tell him.

The moment she made it to his room upstairs, her heart dropped when she heard soft groaning and moaning. From the cracked door leading to Packs room, her heart dropped when she saw him making love with another girl from her high school. He was fucking her from behind…hard.

Distraught she pushed the door open and walked inside. "Packs, what are you doing?"

Packs climbed out of Stephanie's pussy and they both covered their bodies with the sheets. "What are you doing here, baby?" he said trying to appear normal. "I…I thought you had that test today. Remember you told me you couldn't come over. I was just chilling with Stephanie."

"Chilling? What the fuck is really going on?" Tears fell down her face. "I don't understand, how could you do this to me?"

"I don't know what's going on right now," Stephanie interrupted. "Are you broken up with her or not? Because you told me it was over."

"No," Claire responded, "so you need to get the fuck out of here now before I go off on you."

Stephanie quickly got dressed, and eased past Claire who was standing at the doorway with clenched fists.

"I'm sorry, Claire. I mean...I didn't know you were coming. That bitch didn't mean nothing to me."

"I hate you so much right now, Packs."

"I know you do, and I'm seriously sorry. Had I known you would've seen me like this, I would've never—"

"Gotten caught?"

"Yes, gotten caught," he said no longer feeling like faking with her. Besides what could he say? He was caught with his dick inside of the girl's pussy. "The fact of the matter is I'm tired of having sex only when you want to. What about me? What about when I want to be held?"

"Packs, I didn't want to tell you this, but I couldn't have sex with you often because I'm pregnant and get sick quickly. Aren't you happy?" she smiled.

"What the fuck you mean you're pregnant?" he hopped out of bed and jumped into his sweat pants and t-shirt. "I'm not understanding."

"I didn't mean for it to happen, Packs but it did. Please forgive me for my part in all of this."

"But you said you were on birth control. So what...did you lie?"

"Not exactly. I was afraid to tell my mother that I needed them. I didn't want her to know I was having sex, so I never got them."

"That baby is going to die in your fucking stomach." He yelled. "Do you hear me? If you have it, it will die! Because, I don't want no fucking kids. I'm going to college, and I'm going to be somebody in life. Having a fucking baby won't do nothing but hold me back and slow up my grind. So if you want a baby do it on your own!"

Angry, Packs stormed out of the house and jumped into his car. Claire followed him downstairs and begged him to calm down. He wasn't paying her any attention. Instead he backed out of the driveway so quickly, that he didn't see the garbage truck that was on its way to collect the neighborhood trash on his block. The massive green truck rammed into Packs' Range Rover so hard, his body flew out of the passenger side window where he died instantly.

A week later, Claire had a miscarriage.

←—————————————————————————→

Later that night, while Bobbi and Claire were in bed, Packs came to her again. Although Bobbi was snoring, Claire was wide-awake, because her mind wouldn't let her rest.

"Hi, Claire," Packs said stepping into her bedroom.

She turned around and looked at Bobbi who was still asleep. Then she focused back on him. "Hi, Packs."

"She's not good for you, you know," he nodded at Bobbi. "You can still come with me if you want. You got pretty close that day when you tried to commit suicide. If you try harder it will probably work this time."

"I want to live now, Packs," she whispered, "besides she needs me."

He smiled at her. "I'm going to go now. But this time I won't come back unless you are ready to come with me. Okay?"

"Okay." A tear fell down her face.

She missed him already. But, the complete ending of their relationship, marked the beginning to a new one. At least she hoped so.

EPILOGUE

The sun beamed on Bobbi who was in the car talking to her boyfriend. "Last night was real, baby," Reds said to her. "The way your body felt against mine, and how tight that pussy is." He exhaled. "Damn, you felt so good."

"Then why do I get the impression that something is wrong?"

"It is, Bobbi. I mean, I'm starting to want a little more."

The smile on Bobbi's face was so wide her face felt stuck. Just a year or so ago, Reds had thrown her out of his apartment, and wanted nothing to do with her. And now he was practically begging to be in her life. And considering she actually gave birth to his child, even though it was believed she was pregnant by Vyce, things were working out in her favor.

"I want a little more too, and the moment I can give you that I will." She sighed. "It's just that my life is so complicated right now. And I'm afraid if I told you what's going on, you wouldn't understand."

"Try me."

For a second she contemplated telling him that she was in a relationship she didn't respect, even though it was beneficial. Claire did everything for her four-month-old little boy Crandon. Because of Claire the only thing Bobbi had to do in the morning was kiss her baby on the cheek and bounce.

If she left Claire for Reds, all of the responsibility would roll back on her, and she wasn't ready to be a full time mommy. Not to mention Reds may not want anything to do with her anymore, since one of the things he liked was that she could pick up and go at will. Even though Reds knew she gave birth to his baby, he didn't bother to ask to see him. It was all about Bobbi, and what she could buy him.

"I don't want to come down on you with my problems right now, Reds, just know that sooner or later, no matter what, we will be together."

"I hear you, ma," he said with a slight attitude. "But look, I'm about to shoot some hoops with my man. I'll get up with you later."

Annoyed with having to put him to the side, for someone she didn't love, Bobbi spent a few more seconds in her car before going into the house. When she had enough nerve, she walked inside, and as usual, Claire had everything in order and the house was immaculate. The baby was quiet.

"Hey, baby," Claire said kissing her softly on the lips. "The baby is sleep and I ordered out so you don't have to cook tonight."

"That's good," Bobbi responded, trying to hide her attitude from the super sensitive Claire. "You mind if I take a nap?"

"No, go ahead, Bobbi," Claire smiled. *"I'll talk to you when you wake up. Everything is straight here."*

As Bobbi walked into the room Claire called her mother. She told her how happy she was and how life was finally looking up for her. But once again, Ricky made it her business to keep shit real.

"Claire, you have to be careful with your emotions. Sometimes the picture you see may be turned upside down."

"You can never let me be happy can you?"

"I always want you happy. But I also want you to be smart too. Time will tell if your situation will be happily ever after or a horror story in the making."

←————————————————————————→

At Tya's House In Delaware

Tya opened the door when she heard her guest knock. She couldn't believe how handsome Vyce was after all this time. When she looked behind him, she saw that a brand new silver Maserati sat on the curb in front of her Delaware home. She could see as usual, that he is doing quite well for himself.

"Thanks for coming over," Tya said allowing him into her home.

He walked inside, and tried to hide the hate he felt for her inside of his heart. She betrayed him, and got up with some bitches she didn't even know, after eve-

rything he did for her. And, the reason she lived so luxuriously was because she helped Bobbi and Claire rob him and for that he would never forgive her.

"You know I had to come see you Tya," he said kissing her softly on the cheek. "I missed you, and I'm glad to hear you missed me too." He sat on the sofa. "Where's the baby?" he asked looking around the house. Everywhere he turned a toy sat.

"At a friend's house."

He nodded. "I see, I see," he paused. "So let's cut the shit. Start by telling me everything that happened when they robbed me."

"Everything?"

"Yes, and don't miss a thing, my sweet baby."

OFFICIAL LAUNCH

7.27.13

Mean Girls Magazine will offer women the opportunity to reach their full potential in all aspects of their lives, whether it be body, mind or soul. We believe that it's great to embrace your body no matter what shape or size. We believe that the color of your skin doesn't depict how beautiful you are inside or out. We believe it's good to be in tune with your sexuality, and not feel afraid to express yourself in the bedroom. We believe that your dream job may not necessarily involve a nine to five, and we are excited about showing you new and exciting opportunities to launch your career or business. We understand how it feels to be brokenhearted and excluded by those you love, and we support you by accepting you into a community of women just like you.

Mean Girls Magazine is not about being angry, bitter or hateful. It's about being your best, and developing an art of rebellion against all those who mean to step in your way.

FOLLOW US:

Facebook: Mean Girls Magazine
Twitter: @meangirlsmag
Instagram: @meangirlsmag

Sign-up for updates on our website

www.meangirlsmagazine.com

EXTRA RAUNCHY
CHILDREN OF THE CATACOMBS
T. STYLES
NATIONAL BEST SELLING AUTHOR OF *RAUNCHY*

By SHAY
HUNTER

Tranny
911

A NOVEL

CARTEL PUBLICATIONS
PRESENTS

The Cartel Collection
Established in January 2008
We're growing stronger by the month!!!
www.thecartelpublications.com

Cartel Publications Order Form
Inmates ONLY get novels for $10.00 per book!

Titles	*Fee*
Shyt List	$15.00
Shyt List 2	$15.00
Pitbulls In A Skirt	$15.00
Pitbulls In A Skirt 2	$15.00
Pitbulls In A Skirt 3	$15.00
Pitbulls In A Skirt 4	$15.00
Victoria's Secret	$15.00
Poison	$15.00
Poison 2	$15.00
Hell Razor Honeys	$15.00
Hell Razor Honeys 2	$15.00
A Hustler's Son 2	$15.00
Black And Ugly As Ever	$15.00
Year of The Crack Mom	$15.00
The Face That Launched a Thousand Bullets	$15.00
The Unusual Suspects	$15.00
Miss Wayne & The Queens of DC	$15.00
Year of The Crack Mom	$15.00
Familia Divided	$15.00
Shyt List III	$15.00
Shyt List IV	$15.00
Raunchy	$15.00
Raunchy 2	$15.00
Raunchy 3	$15.00
Reversed	$15.00
Quita's Daycare Center	$15.00
Quita's Daycare Center 2	$15.00
Shyt List V	$15.00
Deadheads	$15.00
Pretty Kings	$15.00
Drunk & Hot Girls	$15.00
Hersband Material	$15.00
Upscale Kittens	$15.00
Wake & Bake Boys	$15.00
Young & Dumb	$15.00

Please add $4.00 *per book for shipping and handling.*
The Cartel Publications * P.O. Box 486 * Owings Mills * MD * 21117

Name: _____

Address:_____

City/State:_____

Contact # & Email:_____

Please allow 5-7 business days for delivery. The Cartel is not responsible for prison orders rejected.

Personal Checks Are Not Accepted.

22898134R00125

Made in the USA
Lexington, KY
18 May 2013